A BLACK DOG BOOK

HEIR

OF †HE DOG

Book 2

HAILEY EDWARDS

Copyright Information

No part of this book may be reproduced in any written, electronic, recording, or photocopying without written permission of the publisher or author. The exception would be in the case of brief quotations embodied in the critical articles or reviews and pages where permission is specifically granted by the publisher or author.

Heir of the Dog
© 2015 by Hailey Edwards All rights reserved.

Edited by Sasha Knight
Cover by Damonza

Interior format by The Killion Group
http://thekilliongroupinc.com

THE BLACK DOG SERIES

CHAPTER ONE

Flaming red hair. *Check*. Pasty white skin. *Double check*. Breath like a slaughterhouse in July… I inhaled deeply then wrinkled my nose. Yep. *Houston, we have a troll sighting*.

Now would be a great time to have a partner. Too bad mine was an *ex* in every sense of the word.

Buzzing at my ear preceded a manic giggle as a drunken sprite landed on my shoulder and dry-humped my earlobe. *Gross*. I thumped him in the stomach and sent him tumbling through the air. Four of his buddies zipped past me, whooping with amusement.

Yeah. Real funny. Pick on the marshal. Pests. Sprites were the fae equivalent of mosquitoes, and the town of Wink, Texas was infested.

My flicker of inattention cost me. The troll had gained more ground.

I tugged on the cuff of my glove from habit then tightened my grip on my satchel and followed my mark deeper into the crowded back streets heading toward the O'Leary Bazaar, a nightly street fair held by fae vendors, mostly Unseelie, where you could buy anything your heart desired as long as you were willing to sell your soul to afford it.

No refunds or exchanges.

"Love charm for the pretty lady?" A damp palm grasped my wrist. "Find a man—fall in love."

A trow, a bowlegged woman with a gangrene complexion, jerked me a step toward her booth. Leather bags hung from twisted cords around her neck. The one she jangled in my face boasted a red anatomical heart on its front. As its innards tinkled and its spell awakened, the bloody outline pulsed.

Shrugging free of her, I wiped her slimy residue off my skin and started walking. "No thanks."

The last thing I needed was a man. My heart was still mending from my last breakup.

"Two coppers for the charm," the trow cried. "Pretty lady. Charming lady needs a charm."

I shouldered through the crowd until a head of flame-bright hair came back into view. Bodies parted to ease his brisk passage then clumped together to slow my pursuit. Unseelie solidarity. Nice.

"Charm." That same toad-skinned hand closed over my arm. "Lady needs a—"

Gritting my teeth, I spun toward the trow and noticed the cloudy pink sweat dotting her forehead and dribbling into murky eyes frantically darting between my face and some point past my shoulder.

"Trows," I said thoughtfully. "They're troll cousins, right?"

Her answer involved peeling her eel-skin lips from her ichor-stained teeth and hissing at me.

"We can finish this later." I scanned the street until spotting a flicker of ginger bobbing over the sea of inky-haired sameness. I bolted in that direction as pain razored across my forearm. Dark blood welled and glistened in the furrows the trow had raked in my flesh, but I healed before a single drop fell.

"Finish this now," she growled. "Pretty lady."

"Fine." I was closer to the troll than I had been all week, and I wasn't leaving the bazaar without him.

I raised my left hand, let the trow see the shimmering wards stamped into the black leather glove I wore, let her wonder what all those bindings meant. And then I showed her. Murmuring my Word, I sensed the protective magic locking the glove at my wrist relax. I removed it and flexed my fingers.

Runes covered my skin from wrist to fingertips, casting a soft peridot glow around my hand.

Her rheumy eyes flared. "*Cú Sídhe* whore."

Every person on the packed street craned their necks. Mouths fell open. Bodies shuffled the hell out of my way. No one spoke. They barely breathed while I strolled the narrow gauntlet they formed, taking time I didn't have so all saw the markings, my birthright, and understood what they meant.

Sometimes it paid having Macsen Sullivan for a father.

Ahead of me, the troll glanced back. His bone-white face contrasted with his scalding hair. Stark blue eyes pierced mine. Freckles crawled like ants over his bulbous nose. His teeth, when he smiled, were so much worse. Square pegs, each thicker than my thumb and made for grinding, edges too dull to slice through flesh.

Trolls were fond of chewing their victims to a squishy pulp without breaking the skin. They cut off the head and rolled up the corpse starting from the toes, the same way humans used a tube of toothpaste, squirting out the goo then discarding the empty wrapper in the nearest trash bin.

Grinning, the troll licked his lips. He flipped a table then darted behind a row of booths. When he bolted between two buildings, I broke into a sprint. If I lost him now, I might not get another chance, and I wanted that bonus.

Magic sucker-punched me when I reached the mouth of the alley. No subtle push here. This was a seasoned uppercut while your head was turned. Usually charms like the one I sensed made the location emit *nothing to see here* vibes that spun most folks on their heels. This one blared *fuck off*.

With my head reeling, I braced my bare left hand against the nearest brick wall and shook off the oily threat permeating my senses. Entering the alley alone was a Very Bad Idea, but I didn't get paid to let fae eat humans. Our race was a nibble away from discovery as it was. Both Seelie and Unseelie houses agreed if the fae had to come out, they wanted the big reveal to be on their own terms. Having an ass-ugly troll with people stuck in his teeth for their poster boy? Probably not the smoothest move in the campaign to convince humanity our races could coexist in harmony.

That first step into shadow made my bones creak. Pressure built in my ears until I swallowed to pop them. Runes on my hand provided the only light, a faint green glow. Given tonight's full moon, I chalked the pervasive darkness up to black magic. Someone had gone shopping tonight.

"Smells of dog, it does," the troll's thick voice boomed. "What business does it have with I?"

Paper crinkling on my left made me squint that much harder. "Are you Quinn O'Shea?"

"Aye." He crushed something underfoot, closer to my right.

He was circling me.

I raised my palm, hoping to distract him with the immediate threat while I tugged a daylighter flare out of my satchel. "In that case, O'Shea, I bet you can guess what I'm doing here."

Hot air blasted my nape as his damp nose snuffled me. "You're Black Dog's get."

I suppressed a shudder. "That's what they tell me." I had never met the guy myself.

"Black Dog knows I." He exhaled near my ear. "Thinkin' he won't want it to hurt I."

"The conclave sent me." I twisted the cap off the flare. "My father has nothing to do with this."

"It has Dog's black hair." His chuckle slithered over me. "Does it have Dog's black heart?"

I was nothing like Mac. Our magically radioactive left hands were the only things we had in common, not that I had ever seen his to compare.

"The conclave bids you come with me of your own free will to stand trial."

He chuffed. "Don't much like I's odds if I goes to court."

"If you're convicted of the murders—" and we both knew he would be given his starring role in the convenience store surveillance video, "—you can appeal the verdict. But if you don't report, and if you really do know my father, then we both know what happens next."

"It don't have the power." The troll grunted. "It wouldn't be set loose here if'n it did."

"Last chance." I gripped the flare with one hand and its cap in the other. Each flash of my runes telegraphed my movements. No hope of concealing them. The glow didn't come with an off switch.

"Don't fear death." Claws scraped asphalt when he shifted his weight. "Don't fear you neither."

I rubbed the coarse striking surface of the cap against the button on the flare. Nothing happened. *Damn it.* Trolls turn to stone in sunlight. I had planned to identify Quinn, whip out my daylighter flare and then babysit the hunk of troll-shaped rock until the conclave dispatched a unit with a flatbed for pick-up. But Quinn's nasty little charm must protect him by dousing all forms of artificial light, like my flare.

With a sigh, I tossed the worthless daylighter aside. "You aren't coming peacefully, are you?"

His answer was to hook his meaty forearm around my throat and yank me against his chest. My lungs burned while his bulging muscles flexed, crushing my larynx. I dug the nails of one hand into his wrist. Runes eased beneath my skin, shining like beacons, banishing the gloom.

Damp and fleshy, his tongue slid down my nape. The glide of his blunt teeth followed.

A shudder cemented my resolve. *Kill or be killed.* I had a choice to make. An easy one.

I clamped my bare left palm over his thick wrist. "This is going to hurt."

CHAPTER TWO

Quinn's startled bellow when my magic threaded through his veins to his heart was deafening.

My ears rang as much from his screams as the collapse of his charm. Moonlight filtered through the fading tendrils of darkness, casting faint light between the squat buildings sandwiching the alley.

Glittering bones, each one picked clean and most gnawed to splinters, littered the street. Tossed aside like trash to rot among the wet newspapers and crumpled soda cans. Hard to know who or what left those behind. They weren't troll kills. That much was for certain. They weren't fresh kills, either.

Trolls were opportunistic. The odds Quinn had squatted in another fae's territory were high. Yet another use for that blackout charm. Tack it up, say a Word to activate it, and the charm did the rest.

Power that rich could make any spot with a kernel of darkness blossom into an abyss.

One corpse, the girl whose disappearance tipped off the conclave about our rogue troll problem, sprawled in a heap of broken limbs. The toothpaste trick didn't work as well on humans as it did on fae. Poor kid. I hated breaking bad news to parents who actually cared whether their children lived or died.

The troll's wheezing forced my attention back to him. Enough stalling. Time to finish this.

"By the power vested in me as a marshal of the Southwestern Conclave, I condemn you to death for your crimes against humanity." I gritted my teeth until my jaw ached and braced against the coming pain. "Your soul will now be extinguished and your remains claimed by the Morrigan, as is your right as a subject of House Unseelie. If you have sworn fealty to another deity, and if you wish your remains to be an offering to them, speak their name now or forever hold your peace."

I took his silence as consent and willed a pulse of magic through the runes contacting his skin. A heartbeat later, searing heat cut across my jaw, a scalpel-sharp ache zigzagging past my temple and over my scalp. Razors slashed under my skin with every wicked slice my magic dealt O'Shea.

I hated this part, the severing of a soul from its host, the trimming away of the fat of life and the cauterizing of immortality. Fae were built to weather eternity. Few grasped true death in any context.

But we were all tangles of muscle and bone, flesh and blood, heads and hearts, weren't we?

We could all die if the time was right. Sometimes we did even if it wasn't.

I held O'Shea's terrified gaze while the top layers of his skin peeled away from muscle like ripping off an old bandage. I owed him that. I was ending a man's life and could damn well look him in the eye while I did it. The vicious teeth of my magic savaged his soul, rent the tatters of his self and devoured it whole.

Pleasant warmth suffused my limbs, sating the darker part of me who stared at carnage a little too long, watched each death a too closely and enjoyed a soul-induced high just enough to shove me spinning down a shame spiral only one person could stop.

I wish Shaw was here.

No. No, I didn't. Sure he might pull me out of my guilt tailspin, but that meant talking to him, and if he got me on the phone, I knew what he would want to talk about. *Us.* Except there was no *us*. Not anymore.

The troll's pupils had faded to milky white. He was an empty shell suspended by an intricate web of misery. Magic knifed under his flesh, jolting his corpse, seeping out his pores until his skin released with a wet kiss of sound and puddled at his ankles where the pinky-white folds withered into a dried husk.

What remained was a meat and bone sculpture of troll musculature ready for disposal. Time to ring the dinner bell.

Before gloving my hand, I tugged a quarter-size silver medallion from my shirt by its chain and palmed the cool metal. Rubbing a rune-covered thumb across the triskele stamped into its center, I summoned the Morrigan.

A breeze smelling of wood smoke and embers ruffled my hair. A pulse of black magic beat in the air before me. The ball of swirling mist drifted on the breeze. That…wasn't right.

A carrion crow swarm that blotted out the sky then swooped to encircle an offering in a cawing black feather tornado complete with glowing ruby eyes? That was more her style.

This was something else—*someone* else. But who had the balls to claim her feast in their name?

I lowered my hand to my side where its luminescent threat remained visible.

"You summoned the Morrigan." A thickly accented voice throbbed across my skin.

"I did, and you aren't her." The cadence of those words shivered through me. "Who are you?"

"Whoever you want, *a stór*." His chuckle was worse, all buttery rich and inviting. Dangerous.

"I'm not your darling." I raised my left hand. "By whose authority have you answered my call?"

A moment of silence passed. "I am the Morrigan's son."

"The Raven," I breathed.

Her son and heir, Raven, an Unseelie prince. A prickle of unease quivered along my nape. A prince in the mortal realm. What on earth had lured him here? And did the conclave know? They had to, right? The prince must have used a tether to get here, and for visiting dignitaries, that required permission from the Faerie High Court on his side and the Earthen Conclave on this one.

Straightening my shoulders, I gestured toward the body. "Then you are welcome to your feast."

"Who do I owe for this offering?" Amusement throbbed in that nebulous swirl of magic.

"Thierry Thackeray." Not my Name, but a name nonetheless.

"Tee-air-ree." He dragged out each syllable as if savoring the sound on his...well, he had no lips in this form.

"Let me grab this..." I knelt and rolled up the troll's skin, "...and I'll leave you to it." Tucking the proof of death under my arm, I saluted the magic blob. "Enjoy your feast."

Eager to put Raven behind me, I turned on my heel and strode toward the mouth of the alley, tugging my glove back in place. His mother tended to rip off limbs and gnaw on them like chicken wings instead of, oh, I don't know, someone's *arm*. I shuddered and kept on walking. However her son chose to dine, he was doing it alone.

"I will savor every bite." His voice dogged my heels. *"Go bhfeicfidh mé arís thú."*

Until we meet again.

A shiver danced down my spine as I raised a hand in a half wave and kept walking. The conclave awaited my resolution, and thanks to O'Shea's refusal to stand trial, I had a good three or four hours' worth of paperwork ahead of me.

CHAPTER THREE

On the dusty outskirts of Wink, a ramshackle farmhouse slouched on three hundred acres of dried weeds. Or so its glamour led you to believe. Those who knew the Word and braved the gap-toothed front porch were rewarded with entrance into the modern brick office building run by Mable, who was receptionist, secretary and den mother to us all.

Murmuring a Word, I keyed the ward locking the front door of the marshal's office. I stepped inside Mable's domain in time to catch her licking a dollop of honey from a teaspoon before dipping it into her glass of sweet iced tea.

The sight of Mable's lopsided bun sliding down the back of her head always made me smile.

She was a bean-tighe, a housebound spirit. They were one of several nocturnal races of Seelie. Their personal glamours were usually of the cookie-baking, apron-wearing, booboo-kissing grandma variety, but Mable had taken her illusion one step further. She emulated the ultimate grandmother figure. She was a dead ringer for Mother Christmas, if Mrs. Claus had never met a shade of pink she didn't love. And possibly if the North Pole was, in fact, a dude ranch staffed by ten-gallon-hat-wearing elves.

"Knock, knock." I waited while she adjusted her alarmingly fuchsia glasses. "Did I interrupt your dinner?"

"Thierry." Her round face split into a grin. "Always good to see you, sweetie. Come on in."

"I brought you something." I pulled the troll skin from under my arm. "Quinn O'Shea."

"Oh dear." She covered her mouth with a plump hand. "An execution."

"I…" Old guilt tightened my throat until it trapped my excuse. "It was self-defense."

"I don't doubt it." She bent down, opened the mini fridge under her desk and produced a pitcher of iced tea and a glass that matched hers. "Yours is a dangerous job." She poured the syrupy liquid to the brim then passed the drink to me. "Out in the field, anything can happen. You do the best you can to see that justice is served, and then you do whatever it takes to get home in one piece."

The miserable tightness making it hard to breathe eased enough that when she passed me a tray of my favorite iced lemon cookies, the smile bending my lips was as genuine as the affection behind it.

She jabbed her finger at the chair across from her desk. "Go on, sit. I'll get the papers together."

"First, I have a gift for you." I reached into my messenger bag, a graduation gift from her, and pulled out a small jar. "Basswood honey."

"Basswood, you say?" She clasped her hands together. "I haven't tasted that variety in years."

"I'm glad you approve." I passed it to her. "I'll bring avocado next time."

Despite being employed by the conclave, tradition dictated a price be paid for the services of the bean-tighe. Mable loved her honey, the more exotic the better. Sucking up to the lady who handed out case assignments was always a stellar idea, but Mable was like family. Spoiling her with rare honey made me happy.

"You are too good to me." She unscrewed the lid, her eyes closing as she sampled it by dipping her pinky into the jar and licking honey from her finger. "Divine."

I dropped into the spare chair and leaned forward, propping my elbows on her desk. Two more cookies vanished while she filled out my bonus voucher and printed the necessary paperwork. Chasing O'Shea must have worked up an appetite. "What do you know about the Morrigan's son, Raven?"

"Not much, I'm afraid. I don't involve myself with Faerie's politics when I can help it." Mable capped her honey and placed it in a desk drawer. "Why do you ask?"

I licked my fingers before remembering where my hands had been. *Ick.* I gulped Mable's lemony sweet brew, swishing it around in my mouth. Brushing my teeth with a palm full of sugar would have had the same scouring effect. "Someone claiming to be Raven showed up when I summoned the Morrigan earlier."

I had been working cases solo for over a year now. Factor in five years of education in the fae private school system, plus sixteen weeks of marshal academy, and my summoning skills should have been topnotch. When I summoned the Morrigan, I expected the Morrigan. Not her next of kin.

"Give me a moment." Mable cleaned her hands with a wet wipe then clacked a few keys on her computer. "I don't see any cross-realm travel paperwork filed under his name—or hers." She glanced up at me. "Did you get a good look at him?"

"No." The cookie turned sour in my mouth. "He appeared as a floating glob of energy."

"Hmm. That sounds like a scavenger to me." She clicked a few more keys. "I'll file a report and let the magistrates know there was a poaching incident. That's the fourth one this week."

"There have been more?" Poaching from the Morrigan was suicidal, so understandably rare.

"Oh, yes." She bobbed her head. "Territorial disputes happen to us all from time to time, and she holds the monopoly on conclave business. I can't imagine the other death dealers are too pleased about that."

I sat back and drummed my fingers on her desk. "So there's no way it was Raven?"

"No." She printed out an incident form and slid it over for me to initial. "It's not possible."

"Are we talking no-way, no-how possible—" a curious note entered my voice as I signed off on an official version of the event, "—or unlikely?"

Breaches rarely happened, but where there was a will, and a powerful fae, there was usually a way.

"Princes are physically bound to Faerie." She took the paper, folded it and stashed it in an envelope. "They have other means of visiting. Astral projection. Cognitive illusions. Those sorts of things."

"I wonder who answered my summons." I swirled the cubes in my glass to hear them clink.

"I can send you copies of the other reports, if you'd like." She reached for her notepad. "If a bounty is placed on him, I'll let you know."

Figuring the sum would be tidy, I grinned. "That would be much appreciated."

"There is particular interest in these incidents," she hedged.

Competition for the higher bounties was to be expected.

"Oh?" I sipped on my tea to get one last cookie down. "Who else wants it?"

"Shaw."

Despite the drink, my tongue turned cotton-ball dry. *"Shaw?"*

"Oh dear. You didn't know." Her brow wrinkled. "Of course you didn't. Why would you?"

"Is he—? Shaw's back?"

"Yes."

"Okay. Well. All right." I set the glass down before my jittery hands dumped it in my lap. "That's good. Great even."

Mable cast me a doubtful look.

"I wonder if the Morrigan knows about the poacher," I blurted to have something halfway sensible to say.

"If she did, she would have killed him by now."

"If he can be killed." Not all death-touched fae could be ended.

"There is that." Mable turned pensive. "You two might consider working the case together. You're the best suited pair for the job."

"For old times' sake?" I asked softly, wincing at the grit in my voice.

"Shaw has seniority," she reminded me. "If he decides he wants the case, I have to give it to him. If you worked together, you could split the bounty."

"I'll think about it." I picked at my nails and stared at her from underneath my lashes. "When are you expecting him back?"

"He ought to check in before dawn." She glanced up then, brows drawn and lips pursed like she had sucked a whole lemon out of her tea glass. Clearly, she wasn't hot for this idea either. "Do you want to wait for him?"

"I— No. No need for that." Heat crept up the base of my neck. "I'll be in my office wrapping up O'Shea's paperwork if you need me."

The last thing I wanted was for Shaw to find me waiting on him like a lovesick puppy.

CHAPTER FOUR

The staccato rap of knuckles on wood brought my head up in time to spot Jackson Shaw lean against the doorjamb in my office. A flannel shirt hung from his shoulders in tatters with the sleeves rolled up past his elbows, exposing vivid crimson slashes across his forearms. More gashes bisected his torso, leaving his abs peeking out at me from under his T-shirt. Dried mud caked his boots, and he smelled of...

I coughed into my fist and reached for a bottle of water. "Is that sauerkraut?"

He shrugged while shutting the door then crossed the room and perched on the edge of my desk. "Don't ask."

"Fine. I won't." I swigged tepid water to wet my parched throat. "What brings you here?"

His gaze jerked from my lips to my eyes. "Mable said you had a proposition for me."

"Um, no." Heat blistered my cheeks. "Well, not exactly."

Fabric tore as he removed his flannel shirt and used it to wipe his face clean. He glanced up and caught me staring. A heartbeat later, the scent of bergamot and patchouli stung my nose, the heady fragrance sinking heavily into my lungs, tingling in my limbs with every inhale until my tender nerves sizzled.

Shaw's voice dipped into a husky register. "It's been a long time, Thierry."

Twelve months. *Twelve*. Too long. Not nearly long enough.

"Don't." My voice sounded as small and pained as a wounded animal. "Just don't."

I dug through my satchel for the vial of smelling salts I kept there. I inhaled until my sinuses burned and my eyes watered. Thank God, the pungent scent still cut through his sultry lure. As to why I kept the vial on me, call me sentimental.

His jaw tightened. "The conclave—"

"—had nothing to do with you rolling out of my bed and right into someone else's." Bitter laughter stung my throat. "Five someone elses."

"Give me some credit." He fisted his ruined shirt in his lap. "I tried."

"Not hard enough."

Being faithful to me had almost killed him. Learning he had been unfaithful? Well, that almost killed me.

Shoving from the desk, Shaw began pacing the room. "Did you want something or not?"

I leaned back in my chair. "Mable wants us to work the Morrigan's poaching case together."

A moment passed between us then, and I knew he was remembering the first case we had worked as partners. We had gone after poachers then too.

He planted his feet and gave me his full attention. "I'm listening."

Leaving nothing out, I filled him in on my visit from "Raven".

"Dealing with a death-touched fae means hazard pay." He considered me. "If we split the bounty, we'll both come out with a nice check."

One niggling doubt kept pecking at my brain. The first rule of investigative work was to rule out the obvious, even if the obvious was impossible. "Mable says Raven can't physically be here."

"Black Dog bound him." He shook his head. "Only he can unbind him."

That was news to me. Mable was right. Shaw was leaps ahead of me in the research department.

I wondered, "What about a spell?"

Incubus or not, Shaw was the best spellworker the Southwestern Conclave had.

"Not likely." He scratched his jaw. "Most spells perform a single function. If Raven projected his likeness, he could converse intelligently with you. If he tapped into the invocation circuit the marshals use to summon the Morrigan, he would hear the calls and could send his magic to consume the tithe. The odds of him crafting a spell complex enough to accomplish both tasks are slim."

I nodded in deference of his expertise. "So poacher it is."

Fragrant spice burst in the air between us, twining through my senses until my body softened.

"I missed this," he said. "Us working together."

I made a noncommittal sound and planted my palms on the desktop.

He seemed to take my grunt as agreement. "I'll email you what I have so far."

"I'd appreciate it." Eager for a breath of fresh air, I rose and crossed the room to open the door. "I'll send you a copy of the incident report Mable filed on my behalf."

He boxed me in, the knob cutting into my hip as he stood there, soaking me up like sunshine. A *zap* of connection jolted a gasp out of me when his fingers slid along my jaw until his palm cupped my cheek.

Thick lashes rimmed his burnished copper eyes, a snare that stole my breath. His sun-kissed skin burned where it touched mine, and I struggled against the urge to lean into that heat, to tuck a mahogany curl behind his ear. The absence of his usual smile left stark white creases in the corners of his eyes and faint bracket lines on either side of his full lips.

Damn him and his stupid lure. Damn me too for being stupid enough to be alone with him.

"We'll make this work." His whiskey-rich voice poured warmly through my ears. "Partners?"

I swallowed hard, tasting him on each swallow. "I should— Mai is expecting me."

His finger traced the line of my jaw, sliding down my throat and across my collarbone until he spread a wide palm over my frenzied heart. Fire lanced from his hand to my soul, searing my chest where we touched. With a blistering sigh, Shaw licked his lips, his voice gone hoarse. "You should go then."

My head bobbled. "I should."

But I didn't.

His head lowered, his lips hovering a breath above mine.

Our almost-kiss was interrupted by a fat pink purse bouncing off the side of his head.

"Boy, you better get back." Mable cocked her arm. "No feeding on conclave property."

"Feeding?" I slurred as Mable swam in and out of focus.

"Out." Mable elbowed Shaw into the hall then hooked an arm around my waist. "Are you all right?"

"Yeah." I let her guide me back to my chair. "Fine."

The lure must have hit me harder than I thought.

She cupped my face and tilted my head back. "I never should have let that sweet talker up here."

My eyes drifted closed. "He's fine."

"No." She shook my shoulders. "He was wounded and hungry, and you were an easy mark."

That jolted me awake. "What?"

If my coworkers started thinking I was easy pickings, I wouldn't last the week. If I wanted to keep running with the big dogs, I had to show them my bite was worse than my bark.

CHAPTER FIVE

I ran down the stairs after Shaw, shoved through the front door of the office building and took the steps two at a time. I hit the gravel and jogged across the parking lot until I fisted the back of his ruined T-shirt. "What the hell kind of stunt was that?"

"You wanted to make a deal. I wanted to heal." He glanced over his shoulder. "Now we're even."

I snagged his arm and spun him around. Both his forearms were healed. The angry slashes from earlier faded to silvery white lines as I watched. "You slurped on my soul without my permission—"

"Not slurped. More like sipped." He wet his lips. "You taste as good as I remember."

Hunger peered through his eyes, sparking heat south of the border I'd sworn to never let him cross again. My nipples tightened, ached. The way his lips pursed promised he would soothe away the sting.

I had taken a step closer to him before warning bells started clanging in the back of my head.

"Keep your metaphysical lips to yourself." I planted my fists on my hips. "Or you will regret it."

"I saw O'Shea, what was left of him." He cocked an eyebrow. "As long as you're feeding, your soul replenishes itself."

So he knew I had just fed and had energy to spare. Too bad he hadn't *asked* me to share.

"How can you be sure?" I raised an eyebrow of my own. "You always eat and run."

"About that." He jingled his keys. "You're interfering with the running part."

"If you're going to be here, then you're going to have to learn to respect boundaries." That or I might have to invest in a Taser. "My office, my body and my personal life are off-limits."

"Off-limits works for me." His head lowered a fraction toward mine. "You're the one making this personal."

A pang in my chest made me think he might be right. What was I to him except a free meal with a familiar aftertaste? I was the one lashing out. I was the one hurting. Same old tune, different dance.

I pressed a finger to his forehead and nudged him out of my personal space. "I've had a long shift. Email me your case files tonight. I'll go over your information tomorrow."

I had turned toward my car when his hand closed over my arm.

A throat cleared behind us, saving me from whatever he might have said to make things worse.

"Shaw," Mable called from the sagging front porch. "Take your show on the road."

"Yes, ma'am." He tipped the brim of a nonexistent hat and let me go. "Later, Thierry."

Mable and I watched him swagger over to a pickup that wasn't his usual black monstrosity. A white printout from the dealership still clung to the window, and an orange price sticker blocked part of the front windshield. This truck was a glossy, sapphire-blue dream come true for someone who drove her mom's hand-me-down sedan with peeling bumper stickers from her middle-school days plastered on it.

Shaw climbed into his new ride, punched the gas and churned up a cloud of dust in his wake.

"Give him a ten-minute head start," Mable cautioned.

Waiting implied Shaw wanted me specifically, when he had made it clear that was no longer the case.

I cast a fond smile over my shoulder. "I will."

"Don't be a stranger." She waved. "Remember, you said avocado next time."

I lifted a hand and started walking toward my car. "I'll remember."

Thanks to the magic of basswood honey, she had given me two more cases to work. Both FTAs, failure to appears, which would keep me occupied for another couple of weeks while Shaw and I tracked the poacher.

Unlike Quinn, whose capture padded my bank account by five grand, these two were worth half that. Half the risk meant half the fee. Yet another reason why tackling the case with Shaw made good financial sense. Factor in the hazard pay, and we would each walk away with four grand. Not too shabby.

As I stabbed the sticky door lock with my Mom of the Year key, a flicker of movement caught my eye.

Trapped beneath the windshield wipers, a silky black feather whipped in the breeze.

Magic stung my fingertips when I retrieved it.

Caw.

My heart leapt into my throat.

Caw.

After scrambling to get inside the car, I jabbed the lock button until the satisfying click filled my ears. With my nose pressed against the glass, I spotted a lone black bird circling overhead.

Three short bursts of old-school rock music blaring from my cleavage made me jump. During the second it took me to pull my cellphone from my bra, the ominous bird vanished. I smacked the steering wheel with my palm, swiped the call icon with my thumb and forced enough false cheer in my voice to choke a horse. "Hi, Mom, I was just about to call. I got hung up at work— What? I'll be right there."

CHAPTER SIX

I pulled into Mom's driveway and sat there, staring through the windshield. A deep foreboding settled around me as hundreds of cawing birds hopped, fluttered, pecked at bugs in the sod and at each other.

Black birds.

Ravens.

My cellphone was in hand, my finger poised to dial Shaw and report the eerie occurrence when curtains moved inside the house. A second later, Mom eased out the front door and darted to my car. Shaw would have to wait.

This morning she wore a yellow swimsuit with a black rose pattern. Her silvery hair was gathered at her nape, but flyaways curled around her face. Her feet left no prints, and her knuckle was dry when she rapped on my window.

I hit the button and lowered the glass, breathing in her worry and the wet-feather scent of her guests. "I can wait if you want to change clothes first."

"No, I'll shower later." She plucked at her straps. "I dried out waiting on you to get here." To soften what almost sounded like a reprimand, she added, "I swam first thing, as usual, and when I finished, I found this. I didn't know who else to call."

Animal control? Except the birds' unnatural behavior was obvious, so of course she called me. Unnatural was my wheelhouse.

"Scoot over, and I'll check it out." Nudging her aside with the door, I stepped onto the concrete beside her and inhaled deeper. Bird dander. Carrion. Poop. But no magic. "It's probably a migration thing."

Liar, liar, pants on fire.

Her lips flattened to hold in whatever comment she almost made.

Screwing up my nerve, I approached the nearest one and nudged its tail with the toe of my sneaker. A normal bird would have bolted before I got that close. This one just blinked round, black eyes at me. That wasn't right. I smelled like a predator. I *was* a predator. The birdbrains should have taken a whiff of me then rocketed into the sky.

When Mom's hand landed on my shoulder, I jumped a foot off the ground and whirled to face her.

Deep wrinkles gathered at the corners of her eyes, and laugh lines mapped her face, but she wasn't smiling now.

Not for the first time, I wished I had her faded denim eyes or the rich auburn hair she sported in pictures from my baby albums instead of Mac's wide green eyes and stick-straight black hair that refused to hold a curl.

"Is this something to do with—" she pitched her voice low, "—your job?"

I bit the inside of my cheek while deciding how much to confide. The Raven theme was too blatant to ignore. This was definitely a case of work coming home with me, but until I knew specifics, I followed our standard operation procedure. I lied. "No, it's not."

"I didn't believe that face when you were nine." She stared me down. "I don't believe it at nineteen, either."

Pretending I wasn't offended—I was a damn good bluffer— I asked, "What time did you spot them?"

Not fooled one bit, she said, "Six o'clock."

It was pushing eight o'clock now. At six, I had been buried nose-deep in paperwork. That put my run-in with the poacher around three. Plenty of time for him to organize Mom's lawn party.

The question was why. Was this a message? A warning? Why target Mom—and therefore me—when Mable said there had been three other incidents?

I dragged a tired hand down my face. "Why didn't you call sooner?"

"I did." She reached inside the shelf-bra sewn into her swimsuit top and brought out her cell. "Hold on."

The habit made me grin. She was the reason I tended to use my bra as an extra pocket instead of breaking down and carrying a purse.

"There." Triumph lit her face. "My calls have been going straight to your voicemail for the past two days. When you finally answered, I almost dropped the phone. I was that shocked."

"What's that smell?" I took a few sniffs. "Did you scramble guilt for breakfast again?"

"I'm your mother." She swatted my behind. "I have a right to worry."

"I turned off my cell." I hesitated. "I was…" *don't say troll hunting*, "…troll hunting."

Her knuckles whitened where she gripped her phone. "Troll hunting."

Mom hadn't known who or what Macsen was when they got involved. Not until I came along and wrecked their relationship.

Half-bloods were either born null, or they inherited a portion of their fae parent's power. That meant Mac had to fess up or gamble that I would take after Mom instead of him. Lucky for us, he wasn't a betting man and left her with a contact number—Mable's, actually.

The slip of paper had gathered dust inside a teacup in Mom's china cabinet until the night she came home from work and found me sitting in the floor in my bedroom surrounded by the corpses of my soulless best friends. They came for my thirteenth birthday party, slept over and thanks to me, left in body bags.

Happy birthday to me.

Before Mom called the cops, she dialed that faded number. Shaw came for me, that's how we met, and he brought marshals with him to clean up the mess. I was bleeding magic I had drunk down so many lives, and Shaw took away that pain with a touch that burned clear to my soul.

A bond forged between us that night. Or I thought it had.

Rubbing a tender spot over my breastbone, I looked up to find Mom staring at me. "Have you had breakfast yet? I was just thinking it was eight..."

"And that the doors are already open at Jose's?" She waved her cellphone at the birds. "Get rid of this poopfest, and I'll drive out to the cantina and pick up breakfast—my treat."

My stomach rumbled at the mention of my favorite Mexican restaurant. "You've got yourself a deal."

"Good." Tension eased from her shoulders. "I'll go shower and call in the order."

Once she returned to the house and shut the door behind her, I dialed my roommate's number.

A sluggish growl answered me.

"You weren't asleep, were you?"

Her low groan earned my sympathy.

"I need your help."

"Whph?"

"Where am I?" I pumped my fist. I had her. "I'm at Mom's. So are like a hundred bespelled birds."

"Hmph?"

"It's a long story. I'll fill you in later."

A long-suffering sigh I took as a *yes* blasted my ear.

"See you in a few." I ended the call and leaned against my car, thinking.

Mom reemerged wearing navy capris, a navy and white striped tank top and matching flip-flops. I waved bye as she slid behind the wheel of her burnt-orange mini Cooper and backed down the driveway past me.

While I waited on Mai to climb out of bed, get reacquainted with her pants and make the fifteen-minute run from our apartment to Mom's house, I snapped a picture of the lawn and texted it to Shaw with the caption *We need to talk*. Then I plugged headphones into my cell and blared Tom Petty and the Heartbreakers' "Don't Come Around Here No More" to drown out all the racket.

CHAPTER SEVEN

About the time I began worrying Mai had fallen back asleep, sharp teeth sank into my ankle, and I yelped. A dainty red fox sat on her haunches beside me. Twitching her bottlebrush tail, she yipped twice while narrowing her large golden eyes on my headphones. Oops.

"Did you have to bite me?" I unplugged and tucked away my phone and earbuds. "Damn it, Mai, that hurt."

She bared pointy teeth as if to say *I'm here, now what*?

"It's not my fault you went running with what's-his-name last night instead of climbing into bed at a decent hour," said the roomie who had been out chasing a bonus check all night.

Her ears flattened against her skull.

"Fine. Here's the deal. We get rid of the birds, and Mom pays us in huevos rancheros and fajitas."

Counting on Mom to over-order, I figured I would split my take with Mai.

Mai huffed out a gusty sigh. Her sleek ears swiveled as the birds flapped their wings or hopped in place, reacting to the predator in their midst. I began doubting they could leave, wondering if they were magically adhered to the grass and if there was an undetectable spell invoked here, until a series of rapid-fire yips preceded a bolt of orange-red fur that pounced into the fray wearing an all-too-human grin.

Utter stillness reigned. Three, two…

Feathers exploded in an upward torrent of frantic corvids desperate to escape the kitsune's jaws.

Mai snapped her jaws then, caught one by its tail feathers and flung it side to side before moving on to her next victim.

Five minutes later, the lawn was clear, and Mai flopped onto the grass panting.

"Good work." I walked over and stroked her head. Her fur was warm silk under my fingers. "You should get changed before Mom gets back. She's had enough excitement for one day." After dealing with the birds, if she caught Mai mid-shift or just plain naked, she might flip. I went to the fence and let Mai into the backyard. "The patio doors should be unlocked. I've got spare clothes in the bottom of the bureau in my old room. Take whatever you want."

With an imperious flick of her tail, Mai hefted herself onto her feet and trotted past me.

By the time Mom returned with breakfast, her yard would be back to normal, making it easier for her to pretend I was too. She never asked me for specifics on Mai, so I never confided in her that my best friend was a kitsune, an ancient breed of fox shifter, who shared my love of the nightlife and steaks with plenty of moo left in them.

Mom needed Mai to be an average young woman of Japanese descent. Not another fae like me.

So we all faked it.

Sometimes, even if it was a lie, it felt nice being normal.

After eating with Mom, I gave Mai a lift back to our apartment. With our bellies full of fajita, I proclaimed it siesta time. I got one foot through the door before Mai kicked off her borrowed flip-flops and faced me.

"Is there something not feathery you'd like to talk about?" She set her hands on her slim hips. "Before you even consider lying, you should know I smell his lure all over you."

Busted. I shut the door and slumped against it, brought my keys up and used one to scratch off my flaking nail polish. "Shaw's back."

"And?"

I blew glittery flakes from my thumb onto the floor. "We bumped into each other this morning."

The urge to caress the still-tingling spot where he had fed was an itch in my palm. I resisted because the last thing I wanted was anyone's pity.

Just as I feared, Mai's warm brown eyes softened. "How awkward was it?"

"As awkward as you can imagine times two." I hung my keys on a hook by the door. "We talked. We've established boundaries that should prevent any more black marks on either of our records." I tugged down my ponytail and massaged my aching scalp. "We can make this work."

"Yes," she added her support, "you can."

"We have to." Might as well put it all out there. "We're working a case together."

A slow whistle slipped past her lips. "The magistrates didn't waste time pairing you back up, did they?"

Magistrates. Right. They didn't know our breakup was the reason Shaw had transferred.

"It wasn't official." I mumbled, "It was voluntary."

"In that case…" She ducked into the kitchen and returned with two bourbon glasses filled to the brim with smoky liquid. "Tell Auntie Mai all about it."

I accepted the glass with a grateful nod, took a deep pull of the crisp, fermented drink and sighed as warmth spread through my chest. "Sweet Dreams?"

We plopped down onto the red brocade couch Mai had inherited from an older sister.

"Yep." She drained her first glass with a hiccup. "Brewed by narcoleptic pixies under a full moon."

I snorted.

Rumor had it drool from sleeping pixies gave the wine its special properties. I didn't care. What mattered to me was its subtle sleep enchantment would burn clean through the night— or the day in our case. A few sips took the edge off, weighted your eyes and fuzzed your mind. Tossing back a full glass was like cutting lines and snorting dust straight from Mr. Sandman's personal stash.

Shifting toward me, Mai poured herself another. "Still waiting here, Tee."

One more sip to wet my lips, and I spilled the gory details of my day. O'Shea. The poacher. *Shaw.* I wrapped it all up at the point where I called her to come help me at Mom's.

"Just remember you're not a trainee anymore, you're a full-fledged marshal." Mai ran a finger along the rim of her glass. "Shaw has seniority, and the conclave bylaws are all in his favor. If you two bump heads—or anything else—you're the one they'll reassign this time."

Coming off a recent transfer, even a voluntary one, meant he was ineligible.

"I know, I know."

"At least you have romantic drama." She sank lower into the cushions. "I got nothing."

"Nothing?" My head jerked toward her. "You've gone out every night this week."

Her eyes went liquid. "He failed the test." Grabbing my glass, she drained it too.

Fail a kitsune's test, and you lost her respect. One and done, it was over. No second chances.

"Ouch." I winced. "I'm sorry. You really liked him, huh?"

"He was a nice guy," she slurred. "A goblin, but the hot kind." She wiped the back of her hand across her mouth then fingered her lips like they had gone numb.

"Another goblin?" That made three in as many months. "*Labyrinth* much?"

She held up three fingers. "Two words—codpiece."

"That's one word." I pried the glass from her hands before she dumped it on the carpet.

Mai had an unholy obsession with eighties fantasy movies. *Labyrinth* was her favorite. She was madly in lust with David Bowie's character, Jareth the Goblin King, who was famous for his tight tights, smoldering stares and a very, *ahem,* generous codpiece.

Her head fell back while she twisted silky chestnut strands of hair around her pinky.

"Goblins are..." She stabbed a finger toward the ceiling. "They're hot."

"Uh-huh. Sure they are." I clapped my hands. "Okay, time for all foxy ladies to go to bed."

The noise spooked her, and the next thing I knew a heavy-lidded red fox lay curled on top of Mai's clothes.

Tempted as I was to move her to her own bed, she hated being carried as a fox, and I hated getting bitten even more. Guess she was crashing on the couch. I left her pawing a shirt while she nested.

"Sleep tight," I called on the way to my bedroom.

The bathroom earned a covetous glance from me as I passed. I ought to shower. I reeked of black magic, troll and worst of all, Shaw. But my feet were on autopilot, and the wine was telling me that my bed sure looked good from here. A shower could wait. First I needed sleep to dull the night's sharp edges.

My shins hit the mattress, and I flopped face-first onto my bed.

Bump. Bump. Bump.

My eyes closed long enough to burn when I rolled over and opened them to glare at the ceiling. Must be moving day for the upstairs neighbors. Great. Perfect timing. Today of all days. Working third shift in a first-shift world sucked.

I shut my eyes and thought peaceful, soothing thoughts until sleep teased the corner of my mind.

Nope. Heavy footsteps tromping overhead jarred me wide awake.

"Can't you stomp any louder?" I fisted my pillow and flung it at the ceiling. "Not like I'm trying to sleep down here."

A chair scraped over the floor. Then blessed silence.

I closed my eyes, pressed the pillow over my face and breathed in the scent of mountain spring fabric softener.

Caw.

I jerked upright, and the pillow dropped onto my lap. Across the room, a large black bird hovered outside the glass. Its eyes were ruby red and sharp as the talons clenching the narrow windowsill. Its massive wings flapped as it struggled to perch. When it settled, it tapped the glass with its thick, weathered beak until I slid out of bed and eased toward the window. With glass between us, I could act brave even though my fingers shook when I tested the sturdy lock.

Reassured, I crossed my arms. "Who are you?"

The bird tilted its head to and fro, examining me. Its bloodstained gaze flickered to the latch.

"That's not going to happen, bird boy."

Some things, bad things, required an invitation to enter your home. Grant permission once and they never had to ask again. Rescinding the offer was difficult and, in some instances, impossible.

I tapped the glass in front of his face. "What do you want?"

His squawk made my ears ring as he hopped from the ledge and glided out of sight, taking any chance of me sleeping along with him.

CHAPTER EIGHT

A text from Shaw woke me five minutes before my alarm buzzed.

Yes, we do.

Three words. That was it.

Unimpressed with how the night was starting, I took a scalding shower and dressed for work. After three powdered donuts, I stopped growling. Of course, that might have had something to do with the five cups of coffee I washed them down with before texting him back with a mood appropriate emoji and thumbing through the FTAs Mable had assigned me.

After an hour passed without a response from him, I turned off my cell, grabbed my keys and messenger bag, and headed out the door. I might as well earn some easy money while I waited.

A quick drive across town brought me to one of those Happy Planet Recycling Centers popping up all over southeast Texas. The owner, Mathew Davis, was my fugitive for the day. Davis was a registered hobgoblin, a trickster fae, who got his kicks slathering on glamour and fooling humans into thinking he was one of them. Usually hobs were harmless pranksters, more of an annoyance than a real threat. But Davis had a mean streak. According to his file, he preferred shenanigans his victims didn't survive to laugh off.

Oh joy.

With a recycling empire at stake, Mable was betting he would come peacefully.

Hey, a girl could dream.

I stepped inside Davis's flagship building and into some kind of freakish after-hours' party.

A portly nude hob zoomed past me riding a scooter. I wrinkled my nose. "You've got to be kidding me."

"Watch out, toots." He shook his gnarly fist at me. "You're standing in the middle of the track."

Glancing down, I spotted the dotted and dashed chalk lines of a racetrack under my foot.

A second hob shot past wearing goggles, followed by a third and fourth wearing nothing at all.

I found somewhere less nauseating to look and called out, "Mathew Davis?"

One of a dozen hobgoblins—sans glamour—skidded to a halt with the plastic bottle he had been using as a bat raised over his head. Each of his ears was larger than my whole hand. His eyes were a dazzling shade of blue, his skin a grayish warty hide with thick purple hairs sprouting down his arms. His head reached my waist. His stomach was round and taut, his arms spindly and his knees knobby.

"Mathew Davis." He leapt from his scooter and danced a little jig. "At your service."

"Hi, Mr. Davis." I avoided eyeing his free swinging bits. "I'm Thierry Thackeray, the marshal assigned by the conclave to work your case."

The other hobs sucked in a collective gasp and scurried like roaches into the darkened corners of the massive warehouse. Their chattering made it difficult to hear what Davis said next, but whatever it was sent waves of hysterical laughter crashing through the room as the other hobs bum-rushed me.

Before I could react, they knocked my knees from under me and hefted me up on their bony shoulders. The nearest male whacked my forehead with an empty two-liter bottle similar to Davis's.

Davis executed a perfect back handspring, landing on a fellow hob's shoulders and cinching his sinewy thighs around the poor guy's head. Fisting the red tufts of hair curling out of his friend's ears, Davis guided his mount—who neighed at me—toward a newly chalk-lined section of concrete floor.

"Come back later, lassie." Davis smacked his mount's ass with his bottle. "I'm busy just now."

The sea of hobs washed me past Davis and right out the rear bay door. They tossed me from the dock, where trucks dropped off containers, into a metal box stuffed full of cans waiting to be crushed. The impact knocked the breath out of me.

Metal groaned and casters squealed. I tilted my head back as they slammed the rolling bay door shut behind me.

"I could make them pay for that."

The simple offer hung suspended on a rich breath of wood smoke.

I bolted upright as cold sweat drenched my shirt. "Who's there?"

No one answered.

I shoved to my knees inside the shifting container. "I said—who's out there?"

"Didn't you get my text?" a graveled voice called.

The tension pinching my chest eased enough I could breathe again. "Shaw, texting someone *Yes, we do* is not the same as *Meet you soon* or *See you at seven*."

His hands appeared on the lip of the container. One harsh grunt later, his upper body popped into view. His forearms rippled with muscle when he locked his elbows, suspending himself across from me. He stared down as I knelt on the crinkly aluminum carpet. "What are you doing in there?"

Heat rushed into my cheeks. "How did you know where to find me?"

He found his footing on the side of the container and shifted closer. "I asked you first."

"Congratulations." I tossed a few can tabs like confetti into the air. "Your prize is…answering my question."

"My phone was off when you sent the picture." His lips twitched. "I texted you earlier, but all I got in response was a smiley face flicking me off with one hand while drinking coffee from a mug in the other."

Eyes wide, I tried for innocence. "My thumb must have slipped."

"I figured."

"You should have texted me back."

"And risk your thumb slipping again?"

I lifted my chin like the thought never would have crossed my mind.

"I had to check in at the office and got slapped with some paperwork while I was there. By the time I called, your phone was punting me straight to voicemail so I got Mable to tell me which cases she pulled for you." His gaze touched on the container. "You weren't at the quarry looking for Burke, so I drove out here."

"I turned off my phone." Fae hearing being what it was, I preferred scouting situations without the risk of a poorly timed ring or buzz. It was a habit I had picked up from him, actually.

"No one else has gotten a house call from this guy. Whoever we're after knows you're a death-touched fae now." He hesitated. "He's probably following you around hoping you'll drop someone else."

I grimaced. Great. My own personal scavenger.

"Until we draw a bead on this guy, I don't want you following up on any leads without backup, okay?"

"Sure." As long as he kept off Mom's lawn. "No problem."

"Grab my hand." He stuck out his arm. "I'll pull you out."

"I don't need your help." I kept wading toward the closest edge. "It's not that deep."

"Suit yourself." He released his grip. A second later his soles smacked the ground.

With no one to watch me humiliate myself, I belly-flopped onto the sticky cans to give my body as much surface as possible, then wriggled my way forward until my fingertips brushed warm metal. I pulled myself up the side of the container and swung one leg over its lip and then the other.

When I let go and fell, instead of hitting pavement, I hit a very warm body.

"Watch that last step." Shaw pressed me against his chest. "It's a doozy."

I squirmed, which got me exactly nowhere. "Put me down."

"All you had to do was ask." He set me on my feet, his hand sliding through my hair. "Hold still and let me..." He flashed a metal tab with a few black strands dangling from it. "There we go." He glanced around the vacant parking lot. "So, you're here for Mathew Davis."

I didn't like the glint in his eye when I nodded a confirmation.

"A case brought me out two years ago." He shook his head. "A hob died here."

Nothing for it, I had to ask. "How?"

"Davis's version of the story was the guy fell into the compacter. The hob's wife saw it happen, and she's the one who called the conclave. She said Davis pushed the guy. They'd been playing that weird-ass form of hobgoblin polo, and Davis's mount—her husband—stumbled over a mallet handle and they face planted. Davis lost the match and, according to her, took the loss out on her husband."

I frowned. "That wasn't in his file."

"Davis was cleared of all charges." Shaw seemed unsurprised. "According to his file, he has no priors. But two guys I worked with at the time had each been out here for minor disturbances."

That meant I could kiss my easy money goodbye. "I appreciate the heads-up."

The straightforward approach had ended with me tossed out on my ass in front of Shaw, who had taught me better, which made the incident ten times more humiliating. Time to reevaluate.

The edge of his lips curved in anticipation of a smile. "I can help, if you want."

"That's all right." I dusted myself off. "I can take it from here."

I took it all right. Three more times I entered the building and three more times the hobs booted me out the door. By the time I stomped across the parking lot to where Shaw sat in the bright cab of his mammoth truck, the fingers on my left hand were itching. When I reached him, he silenced his radio.

He scanned me head to toe. "You're hurt."

I touched my busted top lip, wincing like an idiot. Of course it hurt. Davis had headbutted me, and the wound was taking its sweet time mending. Must be some kind of allergic reaction to hobgoblin.

"It will heal." The scrapes and bruises were already mending. "That is one mean little bastard."

Shaw propped his elbow in his open window and set his chin on his palm. "My offer still stands."

"Good." My shoulders slumped, knowing I wouldn't have to ask outright. "I appreciate it."

"I'll help. I'll even let you keep the bounty..." he opened his door and joined me on the asphalt, "...if you agree to have dinner with me."

"No dice." I backed away slowly. "We just agreed—"

"It's not like that." He held up his hands, palms out. "Nothing romantic. Just business."

"Oh." I squared my shoulders. "In that case, sure, I can do dinner."

He strolled past me, hands in his pockets, grin on his face as he headed for the recycling center.

Shaw called over his shoulder, "Do you remember the first thing I told you about incubi?"

I didn't have to think about it. "They'll say anything to get in my pants."

The scent of patchouli drifted in his wake. "Exactly."

CHAPTER NINE

Whistles and catcalls blasted us as Shaw and I entered the recycling center. I cocked an eyebrow at him, but Shaw had gone bye-bye. Tendrils of mist clouded his pupils until his eyes were white voids. His complexion paled. Veins in his face and neck grew more pronounced, pulsing bright blue beneath his skin. The hand nearest me quivered while bone-white claws sprouted from the tips of his fingers.

A shiver of anticipation tingled through my limbs. Somehow it was a comfort seeing handsome Shaw appearing every bit as monstrous as I sometimes felt on the inside. He looked too normal, too perfect, and I was relieved to be reminded he wasn't. Not at all. He was pure fae, pure trouble…pure temptation.

The first time I saw him like this, bare and real, I asked him out afterward.

Of course, I had been thirteen at the time. He let me down easy by promising we would revisit the topic once I was legal. He had been trying to make me feel better by proving I wasn't alone in my *otherness*. Compared to his chilling transformation, the runes gradually creeping up my arm were only a minor tell that I wasn't one hundred percent human, no matter how much I once wished I was.

Davis kept his back turned until he made his goal then faced us with his makeshift bat raised.

"This is the last time, girlie." He paused while his gaze swept over Shaw. "You look familiar."

A low rumble of sound from Shaw filled the sudden quiet. "You made her bleed."

I'm not sure which of us was more stunned—Davis or me. I'm betting me. I bled all the time. It was an occupational hazard.

"I asked her nicely to come back later." Davis's throat flexed. "You ought to teach her—"

"If you finish with *my place*," I snarled, "I'm going to peel your hide like a moldy banana."

Shaw's lips curved in my direction. It wasn't a pretty smile. It was tinged with hunger and made me desperate to cross my legs or invest in a full-body chastity belt. A chastity suit? Was that a thing?

His attention riveted on Davis. "Apologize."

Davis folded his twiggy arms across his barrel chest. "I won't."

A gentle breeze teased flyaway hairs into my eyes. The earthy scent it carried made water pool in my mouth. When the lure hooked the other hobs, cheers for Shaw grew deafening. Davis swiped his mouth with the back of his arm. His chest pumped harder, his nostrils flaring as he inflated his lungs.

"Shaw." I reached for him. "It's not a big deal. Let's slap a restraining Word on him and go."

Forget handcuffs. Not only were some fae allergic to metals other than iron, they were a pain to keep on hand. It was smarter to use one of the conclave-sanctioned binding Words to subdue unruly suspects than risk lawsuits later. Fae may not be human, but they sure loved the mortal court system.

Where I touched Shaw's arm, those fingertips sizzled. I jerked back and flung my hand until the skin regenerated. This was not good. This was an incubus in meltdown. Grinding my teeth, I grabbed him.

"Can I talk to you outside?" The smell of burning flesh turned my stomach.

Shaw glanced down where we touched, and the fire in his flesh extinguished. "I— Sure."

I looped my arm through his, half dragging him from the building. Partway to the nearest exit, I shot a warning glare at Davis. "You've got five minutes. Say your goodbyes and make your arrangements."

"Five minutes." He bobbed his head while keeping an eye on Shaw. "That'll do."

Damn skippy it would.

Once outside, I ushered Shaw toward his truck and backed him against the rear fender.

"What the hell was that?" I pinned his shoulder. "I'll tell you what it wasn't—*helpful*."

"Sorry." His eyes were clearing. "I wasn't myself back there."

"Is something…?" I wasn't sure how to phrase it, if I had the right to ask. "Are you okay?"

His hand reached up to cover mine. "I'm hungry, that's all."

"You're hungry?" He used to last days between feedings. "You just fed."

His color returned as his jaw took on a stubborn set.

I exhaled through my teeth. Not my problem. His diet was his issue.

"Go eat." I stepped back. "I'll wrap up here." I remembered his offer to let me keep the full bounty. "I'll keep your name off the paperwork."

"I appreciate it." He ducked his head. "About dinner…?"

"Sure." If I gave Davis much longer, he might catch a second wind. "Why not?"

Behind me I heard Shaw climb into his truck and slam the door. The engine turned over, and he sat there idling. I didn't look back, didn't check and didn't ask why he hadn't peeled out of the parking lot.

While Davis was feeling compliant, I went inside and read him his rights, which he recited along with me. *Why, no. That never gets old*. I bound him from inflicting harm or escaping then I shoved him into my car.

Not for the first time, I wished the conclave would assign us take-home cars so my personal vehicle wasn't subjected to bare butt cheeks. I used to tuck blankets over the rear bench seat, but all that accomplished was letting suspects know how gross I found the prospect of their various body parts contacting the fabric. Once they realized that, they made a point of rubbing themselves all over the seat. Now I just let it go. Dripping blood, weeping pus or otherwise leaking bodily fluids? Great. Hop on in and sit on down.

Amazing how little they cared about wrecking my property if I gave the impression I didn't care either. Shutting the door behind Davis, I blocked out all thoughts except those of the bonus I was about to receive. There would be too few zeroes to compensate for this, but I needed the cash.

Lately, even after taking so many crap cases, I always owed more than I made.

I mean, I could tell Mom the truth. That when I hit eighteen and accepted conclave employment, the support payments to her for raising a magically gifted minor had stopped. But she had a newly minted bank note for her car, and she loved it. Losing that income meant she lost the mini Cooper.

I could last a while longer, a few more payments at least.

Mom lost everything when the conclave swooped in and cleaned up my mess. Her home, her career, her friends—her whole life—gone. Her part-time gig at the local animal shelter wouldn't come close to paying her rent or her loan. Since I got her into this mess, the least I could do was keep those support payments going to her, even if they were deducted from my paycheck.

With Mai as a roomie and Mable willing to assign me high-risk cases, I made ends meet for us both. It might not always be enough, but it worked for now. I would worry about later when it got here.

CHAPTER TEN

After leaving Mable with Davis and a jar of avocado honey, I received my second bonus check in as many days to deposit at the bank. Flush with green, I felt zero guilt when I grabbed a pizza from Marco's for dinner. The man was a saint for keeping fae hours even though his restaurant was located on the human side of town. His wife was a banshee, which explained his soft spot for things that went bump late at night and craved hot pie after midnight.

Usually I resisted the temptation to splurge—I had learned the hard way it was either feast or famine with this job—but after my crap day I needed some three-cheese therapy.

At my building, I rode the elevator to my second-floor apartment with the pizza balanced on one forearm and the six pack of ginger beer I almost tasted dangling from the fingers of my other hand. I sneezed as a wisp of scent tickled my nose and brought a flush to my cheeks. Too many fresh smells overlapped for me to get a clear read, but the hairs on the back of my neck lifted.

The elevator doors parted, revealing my hallway...and the incubus waiting by my door.

I scanned the hallway then joined him cautiously. "What are you doing here?"

His shoulder rested against the doorframe, his hair wet and slicked back. His jeans and shirt smelled of the laundry detergent I used while we were dating. Still used, actually. Shaw wearing my scent woke some primal part of me I wish had been left to lie.

His gaze touched on my food. "You said yes to dinner."

I had, hadn't I?

Note to self: Make better life choices.

"I got the files you emailed." I nudged him out of the way. "I haven't gone over them yet."

A somber note entered his voice. "This isn't about that."

I studied him. "If this is about us, dinner is cancelled and your check will be in the mail tomorrow along with an amendment to my statement corroborated by Davis."

Shaw clamped his wide palm on the back of his neck. "This is serious, Thierry."

"Fine." I passed him the beer to free up a hand while I dug the keys out of my pants pocket. "Ten minutes."

"Share your pizza," he offered, "and I'll pay for it."

"You can talk and eat that fast?" I accepted his nod as a challenge. "Deal."

Bent over the greasy box, he inhaled. "Pepperoni and onion?"

"With three cheeses." I twisted my key. "Come on in."

Shaw stood on the threshold with an odd expression in place.

"I give up." I swept my gaze around the room. "What are we looking at?"

"Nothing." He stepped inside and turned a slow circle. "I like what you've done with the place."

Our mismatched furnishings consisted of cherry blossom hand-me-downs from Mai's sisters and cow skull accents from Mom's Gothic Western period. Our theme was a little something I called *love blossoms in the desert*.

"It's home." I led him toward the couch and unloaded the pizza from my arms onto the coffee table. I set the ginger beer on top to make sure he didn't start without me then went to scrub the hob cooties off my hands in the sink. "Mai will be home soon. If you want to keep this private, you better start talking."

He plopped onto the couch, opened a bottle of beer with his keychain and set it on a coaster two feet down the table. "Fair enough."

He didn't make another peep while I dried my hands and grabbed extra paper towels and two plates. I dropped onto the cushion beside him, moved the case of beer and plated us two slices each. One look at his grave expression, and I forced the open beer on him. He looked like he could use a drink, even if this brand was nonalcoholic.

Fae like us rarely drank the hard stuff. Lowered inhibitions mixed with our lethal powers made for a dangerous cocktail. I murmured appreciatively when he cracked one open for me. Sometimes it was nice having a man around the house. Or his bottle opener at least.

"When I left," he began in a subdued voice, "it wasn't for the reason you think."

I bit into a slice, not regretting the charge for extra toppings *at all*. "Oh?"

He sat there holding the bottle, peeling the damp label with his thumb. "I'm dying."

A shocked gasp sucked the pizza down my throat, and I choked until my eyes watered and I coughed up the murderous slice of pepperoni clogging my windpipe. "*What?*" I wheezed.

Concern knitted his brow like he hadn't just dropped a bomb on my head and watched it explode, but he didn't say the words again.

"You can't..." Turned out I couldn't say them either. "You're only what—fifty or sixty years old?"

"Seventy-two," he corrected.

Chills walked on mouse feet up my spine. "What's wrong?"

"I had sex with someone."

I didn't like where this was heading.

"She...fed from me while I was feeding from her."

I shifted uncomfortably. "Fed how?"

"Green light." He continued the methodical peeling of the label. "Palm to my chest."

Memories of that night washed over me, flushing my skin and shortening my breath.

Shaw loomed over me, his hips wedged between mine. I traced the hard curve of his right pectoral with my fingertip before placing my left palm over his racing heart. He slid inside me, growling my name, holding me so tight I couldn't breathe, and then he shouted. Not in pleasure, not in pain, but in horror.

That night desire had ignited my magic. I don't know why or what was different that time from all the others. All I know is instead of sliding off him, my power latched on and fed. Fear I would drink him down, panic that my grim history was repeating, was enough to save him.

That time.

There wasn't a next time. Answers were hard to come by, and I was too scared sex with me would kill him. Turned out I worried for nothing. I found him a week later playing naked Twister with five harpy sisters. He hadn't even locked the door. Who cheats on their girlfriend without locking the door?

The next day I paid a local human witch to spell a leather glove with a Word. No more accidents for me. Not with Shaw or anyone else. The witch had enough fae blood in her family tree to give its branches a little *zing* but was so far removed she was mortal. I could have used a fae, but they live for centuries, and I took comfort knowing my secrets would die with her.

Sick to my core, I whispered, "I'm sorry."

"It wasn't your fault." He brushed aside my apology. "You didn't mean for it to happen."

I hated the twist of hope in my chest, the need to hear his explanation. "That's why you left?"

"That's part of the reason." He drew in a long breath. "I went home. I thought my people could help."

"Did they?"

He shook his head.

I set my hand on his shoulder and squeezed. "Is there anything I can do?"

"Don't." His tone shattered, turned to broken glass and cut its way from his throat. "Please."

The anguish in his voice answered for him. I didn't want to make our situation worse or the debts I owed any deeper, but I couldn't have another innocent's death on my conscience. I had plenty of those already.

"Tell me what to do." I tugged on his shirt when he ignored me. "I want to help."

"You don't understand." Hunger reverberated in his voice. "You're the only one who can."

I slowly broke contact with him. "Why?"

"We completed a circuit, Thierry." His eyes were cloudy white when he looked at me. "I can only feed from you."

CHAPTER ELEVEN

Obligation is the worst burden in the world. The sense you must atone for your sins, the guilt that keeps you up at night. First I wrecked Mom's life, now I might have ended Shaw's. Under different circumstances, I might have joked about my sexual prowess breaking an incubus, but I wasn't laughing now.

Thierry strikes again.

I did this. I broke him. That meant I had to fix him. There must be a way.

I rubbed the back of my arms. "How long has it been since you fed?"

He shrugged, closing his eyes until he regained control. "That isn't why I came back to Wink."

"Why did you?" I bit my lip. "I didn't mean it like—I was surprised is all. Transfers usually last two years."

The longing in his gaze twisted something in my chest. "I had my reasons."

"I'm guessing they involve me since you wanted to meet and talk this out." I struggled to find polite phrasing. "Do you want to establish a feeding schedule or something?"

"No." He shook his head. "Nothing like that."

Aware of what I was offering, I swallowed hard. "Are you sure…?"

"I can't turn you down again, Thierry." He clenched his fists. "I'm not that strong."

"Okay." I wiped my damp palms down my jeans. "Then I'm not sure what's happening here."

"I regret how things ended." He pushed to his feet. "I just wanted to make things right between us."

The misery of his betrayal rushed back in a moment of agonizing clarity, but the memories were fuzzy around the edges, the details faded. The hurt was more remembered than felt these days. Guess I was healing after all.

"We're good." I stood beside him and took his hand. "Also? You're not leaving until you've fed." Flames leapt into my cheeks when his tongue darted out to moisten his lips. "We're not having sex." I rolled my eyes at him. "Take what you need to get through the day. We'll meet up tonight before work and put our heads together, okay? We can figure a way out of this."

Subtle warmth from his palm seeped into my skin, spiraling up my arm and through my chest.

His fingers tightened until his grip hurt. "Ready?"

As I ever would be. "Fire away."

Heat pulsed beneath my skin. The slow draw of energy from my runes into his hand let me acclimate to the remembered sensation of feeding. But the more he sipped, the harder his pulls turned and the weaker my knees became.

A rumbling sound disoriented me. I grasped for his shoulders, but my hand slid down his arm.

With cold certainty, I understood the sound was a growl pouring through his parted lips.

The leash of his control snapped with a roar, and he drank me all the way down.

"I'm calling the conclave if you don't get your ass out of here now."

Mai?

"I'm not leaving until she comes to."

Shaw.

"You almost killed her," Mai screamed. "Touch her again, and I'll shift and chew off your nuts."

"She's coming around." Shaw's voice came from next to my ear. "Thierry?"

I blinked a few times, settling on a hard squint at the overhead light. My limbs felt weightless. I was hollowed out and boneless. My temples throbbed. My tongue was thick and cottony. I ached all over.

He braced a hand on my shoulder. "Can you hear me?"

"Yeah." I rubbed my ears. "You're loud."

"Thank the seven mothers." Mai knocked him aside. "Are you okay?"

"I think so." I waved a hand over my head. "Am I floating? Do I look floaty to you?"

"Thierry?" Mai grabbed my shoulders and shook me. "Do you know where you are?"

Her nails punctured my fluorescent buoyancy, slamming me back into my tender body.

"Judging by the spring jabbing my lower back…" I winced as I repositioned myself, "…I'd say I'm on the couch."

Her grip eased. "Can you sit up?" Ready or not, she gripped my hands and pulled me into an upright position.

Shaw hovered behind Mai, hands shoved into his pants pockets. It didn't help. His tightly balled fists were outlined against the denim in his jeans. His color was high— embarrassed or just well fed?—and he set his mouth in a hard line when our gazes met. No. Not embarrassed. Ashamed. That was so much worse.

"I'm fine." I hoped he read my sincerity. "I'm just tired. I've been running on fumes for days."

His curt nod was all the answer I got before Mai stepped in front of me and cut our eye contact.

"Hello?" Her bright eyes flashed with anger. "I found you passed out and being pawed over."

"It's not what you think." I massaged my temples, but the conga line between my ears persisted.

She set her fists on her hips. "It looked a hell of a lot like you let him feed on you."

"Um." I blanked on a good excuse. "Fine, it's exactly what you think. Can we talk about this later?"

With a disgusted huff, Mai headed to the kitchen. She poured a glass of orange juice, brought it to me and held it under my nose. "Drink this."

On the first sip, I reassessed. "This is not orange juice." It tasted the way burnt rubber smelled.

"There's orange juice in there." She tapped the bottom of the glass. "It's something Mom mixes up for when the kits tire themselves out shifting. If they get stuck furry for too long, they form an unhealthy bond with their furry side. They're at risk of going feral. This gives them a nice boost."

Eyeing the glass, I decided against a boost. "I want to sleep."

"Fine." Mai shrugged. "I'll sleep with you."

I cleared my throat. "You don't have to—"

Too late. Mai was tugging her blouse over her head. Her high heels thunked to the floor, followed by her dress pants. While she stripped within touching distance of a starving incubus, I watched him for signs of interest. There were none. Zero. Zilch. He wasn't sneaking peeks or whiting out or anything.

Even while we were dating, he would slip up and stare too long at passing women. It was the nature of the beast. I forgave him. I understood. It was the touching part that broke me. This—I didn't understand at all.

First his lapse in my office, and then his partial regression at the recycling center. This topped both of those for most eerie incubus behavior ever by a landslide.

A sharp yip brought my attention back to Mai, who had shifted and stood flicking her tail in my direction. She jerked her head toward my bedroom and barked once.

"Give me a minute." I scooted her aside with my foot. "I need to say something to—*ouch*."

Pinpoints of blood welled from the bite mark on my ankle, there and gone, but the pain lingered.

Shaw had taken the hint and stood waiting for me by the door. I walked gingerly to him, keeping an eye on Mai and her pointy teeth. She sank to her haunches with her ears pinned flush to her skull, growling.

I leaned my shoulder against the wall since the room kept shimmying. "How are you feeling?"

His fingers traced the curve of my cheek. "I should be asking you that."

I gave him what I hoped was a pointed look.

His hand fell to his side. "Better."

"Good." I shrugged off the tingles from his caress. "I'm glad."

The awkward kiss he pressed to my temple sent pleasant heat twisting through my chest.

"Night," he murmured, lips brushing my ear.

He stepped into the hall, his gait loose and easy as the tension of the day melted away from him.

"Night," I said to his retreating back. "Tomorrow we block out some time to work on our case, okay?"

A cold nose butted my ankle. Mai stared after Shaw through golden eyes until he stepped on the elevator, before trotting off toward my bedroom. I shut and locked the door then trudged after her.

Nothing had ever felt as good as my head hitting that pillow.

CHAPTER TWELVE

I threw out my arm and knocked an empty water bottle off the nightstand while groping for my cellphone. A push of a button made the display flash and temporarily blinded me, but not before I saw it was three in the afternoon.

Bump. Bump. Bump.

My gaze speared the ceiling. Not again. Another round of knocks and bangs curled my lip. It wasn't the new neighbor's fault I worked nights or that I slept through primetime moving hours. But I was tired and stressed, and we had to coexist for the next year at least, so this had to stop. Now. Today.

Snuffling sounds reminded me for once I wasn't alone in bed. I cracked a grin at the sight of Mai curled up at my feet, in human form, snoring, undisturbed by the racket overhead. Holding her fox shape exhausted her. Once she fell asleep, she often reverted to two legs.

Sliding out of bed, careful not to jostle Mai, I tiptoed into the living room. I gripped the doorknob, forcing my sleep-addled mind to consider for a moment what I was about to do might stir up more trouble than it was worth.

Moment over.

Wearing a sleep-rumpled Pooh Bear shirt and matching shorts, sporting wildebeest hair and shielding the new neighbors from my morning breath—afternoon breath?—with my hand wouldn't make the best impression, but I was past caring how I looked. Or smelled.

The elevator ride up to the third floor gave me even more time to reflect on the possible rashness of my impending confrontation. *Nope.* Still doing it. I had to beg a reprieve. A few hours, a little shuteye, then they could bumpty bump around all they wanted.

Each floor recycled the same numbers, so I walked a straight line to the apartment matching mine. My hand lifted as the door swung open, and instead of wishing him a good afternoon, I almost swallowed my tongue.

A man stood in the doorway. Fae by his scent. By his looks too. No one that gorgeous had an ounce of human blood in them. He was tall. I was five ten and had a view of his chin. Following the curve of his jaw, I slid my gaze across his high cheekbones to meet his eyes. They were black with silver rims around his irises. Infinite. I stared at him, and cold, heartless eternity stared back. I jerked my gaze away. Had to. Before it consumed me.

The rest of him was…not easier to look at…but I couldn't stop gawking.

His hair was black as midnight and hung unbound to his waist. His flawless skin had a grayish cast, but not sickly. Nothing about him telegraphed weakness. He was almost monotonous. A study, not only in the black of his hair or the white of his lips, but in all the varying shades of gray.

He had answered the door wearing low-slung jeans in his bare feet. Even his toes fascinated me.

That I noticed his bare chest last surprised me almost as much as the ornate silver cuffs clamped around each of his biceps. Lean muscle rippled as he moved to cross his arms over the chest I had so openly admired. As my focus traveled down his torso, my gaze got hung up on his hipbones, on how low his pants hung, and the fact not a hint of elastic rode above the line of his faded jeans.

Boxers? Briefs? Commando? Never had I been more invested in a man's choice of underwear.

The man in question cleared his throat.

The fire of a thousand suns burst across my face as I offered him my hand. "Hi."

After a brief pause, he must have decided to allow me skin privileges, because he clasped my hand between his palms. His thumb rolled across my knuckles while the slightest corner of his lips curled.

"Hello," he said, and his words rang through my bones.

An awkward moment passed while I debated how to get my hand back, if I even wanted it back. Some fae, especially older ones, had odd ideas about what such permissions meant. Too late to panic now. I had initiated contact. All the warnings hammered into my head flittered right out the window when I looked at him.

And his window was open. I saw it from here, once I tore my gaze from him and peered into his apartment. His empty apartment. Not one stick of furniture in sight. So what had made all the racket?

"I heard noises," I finally managed. "I thought I would come up and…"

A mocking smile curved his lips. "Introduce yourself?"

"Yes." I gave a test pull on my hand, and he released me.

He rubbed his fingers together as if savoring the sensation. "We've already met."

"I think I would remember…" A flicker of connection locked my knees when all I wanted to do was turn and bolt. *His voice.* I should have recognized it. "You collected the Morrigan's tithe from me."

His black eyes gleamed. "I did indeed."

Wishing I had my cell to call for backup, I demanded, "Who are you?"

"I am the Morrigan's son."

I drew up short. "Fae can't lie."

"Fae tell the truth so well it might as well be a lie," he replied.

Tell me something I don't know.

"Okay, for the sake of argument, let's say you are Raven." I humored him. "What do you want from me?"

"Come inside where we can talk." He promised, "I won't hurt you."

I stared past him and shivered. "Was it just me, or did I hear an unspoken *you don't have a choice* in there?"

Short of tossing me over his shoulder, nothing was getting me inside that apartment.

A wisp of amusement lightened his voice. "I bring news of your father."

Except maybe that.

"That's why you've been hanging around me?"

"It is a matter of some delicacy, perhaps not best discussed out in the open." He pushed the door wider and lowered his hand. "Even empty halls have ears."

"This isn't a trick to lure me inside so you can reap my soul and leave my body for the crows?"

Oh wait. He was the crow.

"No." His laughter rang with silky promise. "You are safe from harm with me."

What I heard between the lines was that he wouldn't personally hurt me, which wasn't the same as protecting me, and it didn't rule out him enticing me into his apartment so someone else could do it for him.

He must have understood my predicament. His first real smile knocked the air from my lungs.

"Thierry Thackeray, I, son of the Morrigan, sworn into service by the Unseelie House, swear that no harm will befall you by my hand or any other's as long as you enjoy my hospitality."

Tempted as I was to nibble, I still didn't take his bait. His vow hinged on him being the Morrigan's son. Twice now he claimed to be Raven. Fae were tricky, but there was zero wiggle room in his statement.

I am the Morrigan's son is a concrete statement of fact. Okay, so, following that logic, this guy must be Raven. How he got here or what his plans were I wouldn't know unless I took him at his word and entered his apartment, which had Very Bad Idea written all over it.

I worried my thumbnail with my teeth. This lead might crack our case and fling open an even bigger one. A Faerie prince here? Without proper documentation? The magistrates would lay golden eggs when they found out.

"I vow I will return you to this spot, where you surrendered yourself into my most humble care, unmolested, under identical conditions to the ones from which you left. Do these terms please you?"

Raven offered his hand again, and this time I sucked in a sharp breath and took it.

He guided me over the threshold into his empty living room and shut the door behind us.

All the other doors stood open. All the other rooms sat empty. "Can I ask an honest question?"

"As long as you don't expect an honest answer."

My head whipped toward him. "Was that a joke?"

"That question is only asked when the joke fails to perform." Raven snapped his fingers, and a faded couch resembling the one in my living room appeared. He led me to it. "Have a seat. I want you to be comfortable." He noticed my preoccupation with his sofa. "Your roommate is sleeping. You are away. I see no reason why we can't use your couch, do you?"

"I— No." There was comfort in the familiar, especially under such peculiar circumstances. "This is fine."

I sat on the middle cushion, amused when a familiar spring poked me in the butt. Raven perched on the arm closest to me. Despite his posture and casual clothes, he evoked this primal fear response in me. As if death were more hideous because of his beauty, and I had zero doubts Raven was a killer.

His stillness unnerved me, made me feel like a field mouse trying to outmaneuver a bird of prey who saw the landscape unfurling for miles but afforded me the luxury of running myself to exhaustion before he swooped in for the kill.

Raven tapped his fingers against his thigh. "Your father is missing."

I sank deeper into the sofa. "What does that have to do with me?"

"He brought balance to the lands of Faerie. Now is a dangerous time for scales to be tipped."

"I can sympathize, but I've never met my father." I shrugged. "I have no idea where he is."

"We are aware of that. We don't expect you to find him. It's more we were hoping you might be persuaded to act in his stead. Only one of his bloodline may take his place, and you are the only known child of Macsen Sullivan." He paused. "We are not without resources. You will be compensated."

Caution lent my voice a sharp edge. "Who is *we*?"

"I speak for House Unseelie."

Another statement. This one more malleable, but I let it slide. "What is their stake in this?"

"Balance must be maintained." Power thrummed in his voice. "It was your father's duty to serve the fae realm and now, as his only child, I offer you his position. If only temporarily."

"You said he went missing. Why are you acting like he's dead?"

"When old creatures go missing in Faerie, it is because they do not wish to be found."

The pressure in my chest eased. "So he might be taking a vacation from court life?"

One year in the field and my job frustrated me. After millenniums of casting irrefutable judgments upon those condemned by the Faerie High Court, of which my father was a founding member, I would be ready for a break too.

Raven cast a meaningful look my way. "He has done so once before."

Right. He took a position once with the Earthen Conclave, spent a few months here and met Mom.

Would she want to know Mac had gone missing? Would she care? Or would she worry he might be here and hadn't come to visit? Maybe this was what Mac did. Maybe he had a thing for mortal women. He wouldn't be the first. I might be the only child of his to appear on the conclave's steps with blood on her hands, but that didn't mean I was the only child he had sired.

The thought of having siblings out there... *No*. Raven said Mac had done this once before, with Mom. Pathetic, I know, but I clung to the childish dream she had been special to him, at least until she got pregnant with me.

I twisted to face Raven. "Why not wait for Macsen to return?"

"It's a delicate time in Faerie, as I have said." He glanced away. "We can't afford to wait."

Unseelie being concerned over the balance in Faerie struck me as suspicious. They weren't all bad, just as Seelie weren't all good, but Unseelie were called *dark* fae for a reason.

"I'll think about it." I pushed to my feet. "My father left this realm before I was born, so you understand why I don't feel any particular attachment to his legacy or any concern for its continuance."

Raven stood as well.

"I'm sorry he vanished," I continued, "but I have to think of my mom, the parent who stuck around and raised me. I'm all the family she has. She needs me."

As powerful as my father was, he had cultivated equally lethal enemies. Mom was under conclave protection, but being Mac's mortal ex-lover, and the mother of his heir, made her a tempting coup for any of them. Especially if I wasn't here to see the law enforced on her behalf.

I liked to believe I could handle myself, mostly, but Mom had no means of protecting herself against the fae.

I couldn't do this. It would be Mac all over again. I couldn't leave her for Faerie.

Raven inclined his head. "I can allow you twenty-four hours to consider your options."

"Do me a favor while we sort this out." I didn't make it a question. "Don't answer any more of the Morrigan's summons, okay?"

"As you wish." He trailed me to the door, pinching a lock of my hair and twisting it around his finger. "As it is, I have taken enough to sustain me."

Unnerved by his familiarity, I glanced over my shoulder. "What happens if I don't go?"

He bent to inhale the hairs caught in his fist. "The houses will declare war upon one another."

CHAPTER THIRTEEN

Raven's offer left me so keyed up, I decided against returning to the apartment. Mai would be waking up and getting ready for work soon. Opting to let her sleep while she could, I shot her a text and told her I was heading in to the office early.

I had solved the case. *Go me*. Fat lot of good it did.

Any doubts I had about Raven's identity had gone up in smoke. He was here. He was real. And his plea implied dire consequences for Faerie if I turned down the Unseelie's offer. I needed to get Shaw's take on this before I involved the magistrates, and I had to involve them. Soon. Say within twenty-four hours.

Once inside the marshal's office, I breathed easier.

"Hey there, sunshine," Mable chirped as I passed her desk. "Are you going after that púca? An anonymous tip placed him at Oak Trail Park ten minutes ago."

I exhaled on a curse too low for her ears. "Have you seen Shaw yet?"

"Yes." She pushed her glasses up her nose. "He came by earlier to pick up a search warrant the magistrates wanted executed before sunup."

Great. So he would be occupied for a while.

"In that case, I'll grab a quick shower and check out the tip on the púca."

Her voice trailed after me. "I don't suppose you—"

"Catch." I twisted and tossed her a square jar of lavender honey. "Let me know what you think."

Her shocked laughter when she caught my pitch made me chuckle.

She picked her spoon off her desk and waved it at me. "I'll do that."

The scent of pine cleaner made me wrinkle my nose when I entered the communal showers tucked into the rear quarter of the marshal's office. It took a few tries, but I managed to remember my combination and pop open my locker where I kept a change of clothes. Five minutes later I was standing under hot spray, ignoring the way my elbow kept banging into the wall of the tiny stall or the knobs jabbing me in the back when I turned to rinse my hair.

Cold air rushed beneath the sheet of opaque plastic and kissed my ankles, raising gooseflesh.

"Hello?" A wispy shadow rippled over the curtain. "Is someone out there?"

A voice in the back of my mind screamed, *This is how all horror movies start.*

Naked chick plus a shower stall equaled a bloody horrible death. Always. No exceptions.

Thanking forethought for getting my glove spelled against water, I whispered my Word and felt the tingle of its magic releasing. Rolling down the material gave me a head start if I needed one. I hoped it wouldn't come to that. I prayed my imagination was in overdrive after visiting with Raven and yanking the curtain open would slam the brakes on my speeding heart.

One. Two. Two and a half… *Three.*

I shoved open the curtain.

Nothing.

The room was empty. No shadow. No freaky cold air gusts. Just naked ol' me.

"Beware the Rook." A gruff masculine voice ricocheted off the tile surfaces, seeming to come from everywhere and nowhere at once. Nails clacked as the rich voice receded. "You are his pawn."

"The Rook?" I snatched a towel from its peg. Slipping and sliding, I skidded after the sound. "Wait."

My right foot shot forward. I tried to regain my balance, hit a soapy patch and went down hard, cracking my head against the slick floor. The overhead lights blurred and spun in my vision.

"Thierry?" Mable called. "Are you all right? I thought I heard something."

I sucked in air to fill my lungs and croaked, "Careful. It's slippery."

All those whirling lights made me dizzy. Shutting my eyes settled my stomach.

"Let me have a look." Mable sounded closer. Her hand eased under my head, searching the base of my skull. "You've got one nasty bump, but you aren't bleeding. Thierry? Dear? What happened?"

"Who else is here?" I managed.

Her warm hands pushed the sticky hair from my face. "In the building or on the grounds?"

"In the building." I opened my eyes. "Someone was in here. He spoke to me."

"He?" Her pencil-thin brows slanted. "There are no male personnel in the building currently."

Bracing on my elbows, I raised my shoulders off the floor. "How about civilians? Fugitives?"

"One fugitive." Mable stood and helped me to my feet. "A fire sprite Marshal Jenkins brought in earlier, but he's already been processed."

"The Rook." I snapped my fingers as the voice's warning clicked into place. "Who is he?"

"The name doesn't ring a bell, dear." She dabbed at the wet spots on her cotton-candy-colored skirt. "You hit your head pretty hard..."

A borderline growl laced my voice. "I know what I heard."

"Maybe it was a sprite." Careful of the mess I'd made, she picked her way toward the window I had forgotten was there. Probably because someone tacked a dressing mirror over it. "It's open."

Open. Of course it was. Why wouldn't it be? All hidden windows should be left cracked before they're covered and forgotten for decades at a time. Whatever. Didn't matter. I knew what I heard. I also knew someone else I could ask. Raven.

I didn't believe in coincidence. First his visit and now this? The two must be related somehow.

"You're right." I cobbled together what I hoped was a convincing smile. "They're such pests."

"They really are." She shut and latched the window. "I wish that banishment bill would get an approval stamp. Faerie can have the little devils back. I moved here to escape that type of nonsense."

Sprites were pranksters. Their idea of amusing ran the gamut from fart jokes to pickpocketing.

Tiny brains, tiny capers. This stunt was outside their usual scope. Someone else was behind this.

More fae than I must know Raven was here. As eager as he was to escort me to Faerie, I was equally sure there were those in both houses content with the status quo.

At the moment, I was too.

CHAPTER FOURTEEN

Sighting a púca meant one of two things. Either you were about to have kick-ass luck, or you were about to get hit with the *sucks to be you* stick. Call me crazy, but black animals conjure grim tidings in my book, and púcas were extreme luck bringers. Either you got the wicked good or the holy-hella-bad variety.

Based on the color of their fur, I was guessing they preferred the latter to the former.

The file on this particular one, Sean Walters, was as thick as my wrist. He was a repeat offender.

Apparently, he liked mixing his mojo. A touch of extreme luck. *We won the lottery!* Followed by a jolt of the worst luck ever. *What do you mean the ticket was fake?* He was just plain cruel. The jerk deserved what he had coming to him.

Rock music blaring in my bra startled birds from the patch of woods I was investigating.

Stealth fail. I hung my head. My mind was not in the right place for this today.

I tugged my phone from inside my shirt, swiped the green icon and whispered, "Hello?"

"Why are you whispering?" Mai whispered back.

"Smart-ass." The wind shifted. I inhaled deeply. *Gotcha.* "I have to go."

"Why?" Suspicion sharpened her tone. "What are you doing?"

With no small amount of glee, I shushed her. "I'm hunting wabbits."

"Fine. Don't be serious." Mai huffed. "But what did you do with the couch?"

"Um, we'll talk later. Bye." I ended the call.

That feathery bastard kept our couch? After digging a notepad from my satchel, I wrote myself a reminder to hire movers, preferably hunky ones, to wrangle the couch back down to our apartment.

A whiff of púca hit my nose, and I bared my teeth. *Here bunny, bunny, bunny.*

After turning off the phone, I tucked it into my back pocket and crept forward.

Judging by the abundance of rabbit pellets in the grass—*eww*—Sean often hunted in the sprinkling of trees bordering the walking track. I got that prowling the track made hunting easier. Most humans were easily duped by the supernatural, and prey ran past you like a conveyer belt of potential victims here.

I even got why he preferred his bunny form to his horse or goat shapes. Bunnies were cute, cuddly and had no human kills on record. But Oak Trail Park was on the human side of town, and his shenanigans were going to get him caught, skinned and deep fried one day.

Hunkered down, I crept forward. Pungent magic led me right to Sean in time to see him jump onto the track, rear up on his hind legs and twitch his pink nose at the next person who passed. The elderly woman paused in her power-walking to coo at him. Huh. Most folks had better sense than to approach wild animals. Sean must be using a charm. Or maybe Púcas came equipped with magical lures, like incubi, minus their sexual vibe.

Wiggling his cotton tail, Sean turned and hopped toward me, attempting to lead the woman into the privacy of the trees.

A mocking caw had me scanning the sliver of open sky visible to me while I crouched in position.

The woman's scream brought me to my feet as a massive black bird swooped toward Sean.

"Unbelievable." I burst onto the track beside her and demanded, "Where's the bunny?"

She pointed upward.

The bird, an abnormally large raven, circled overhead with a limp rabbit clutched in its talons.

"Was he yours?" She covered her mouth. "That poor little fellow."

"No, he was—" I bit the inside of my cheek. "Yes. I was walking him when he chewed through his harness and hopped away." I gestured toward the trees. "I chased him into the open and—"

"I'm sorry you had to witness that." Her hand lowered to clutch the simple gold cross necklace she wore. "Would you like to sit for a moment?"

"Thank you." I eased back a step. "I think I need a minute alone."

Breathe in. Breathe out. Think calming thoughts.

Fluffy clouds. Blue sky. Black birds. Automatic rifles...

No. Bad idea. Deep breaths. Calming thoughts.

Screw it. Raven owed me after this.

Of all the bunnies in all the world, he swooped down on mine.

Back at my sedan, a couple of surprises waited for me. "Do I even want to know?"

Sean the bunny was hopping mad inside a plastic pet crate resting on the hood of the car. His captor held a head of iceberg lettuce and wore an amused smirk while peeling off leaves and poking them through the bars. Sean, for his part, shunned the greens, which amused Raven more.

Raven stood there, still barefoot, but wearing a faded denim shirt tucked into his jeans. Even his hair was tamed. He had plaited it down his back and tied the ends with a blue velvet scrunchie some preteen girl in my apartment building was probably tossing her room to find.

Given Raven's tendency to take what he wanted, one of my neighbors must have also supplied Raven's clothes, which tempted me to ask him for a name to go with the wardrobe. I restrained myself, but barely. Asking was the same as admitting I found his build attractive, which struck me as inviting trouble. The pet carrier intrigued me less, though someone must be searching for Sparky's home away from home.

Before Raven crossed realms, we had to talk about him returning his *borrowed* supplies.

"I got bored." The lettuce vanished from his hand. "This realm is…dull…compared to home."

My eyebrows climbed. "Dull?"

He dusted his hands. "How do you entertain yourself?"

"I read or stream movies on my computer." I paused. "When was the last time you were here?"

His gaze went distant. "During the Wars of Scottish Independence."

Damn.

I mentally adjusted his age. "You don't seem traumatized by modern technology."

Raven's finger cut a trail through the pollen turning my white car sneeze-worthy yellow. He rubbed his thumb and finger together. "Is that how it works in those movies you watch?"

"Yes." I amended, "Not that I believe everything I see on TV."

"Nor do I."

"Wait—you watch TV? In Faerie?"

"It required time to cross the threshold in such a way that my trespass into this realm would not be detected immediately." Raven pursed his lips. "My consciousness was here before my body arrived."

A guy who could literally separate his mind from his body. Nope. Not creepy. At all.

"The black spot. That was you, pre-body?" I considered him. "So your consciousness chilled out in this realm and waited for your body to appear? And you figured while you waited, you might as well learn about our world?"

He nodded.

"Then you upgraded to birds."

Another nod.

"Birds who camped out on my mother's lawn."

His lips parted before he mashed them shut.

"She wasn't thrilled with that. It would be great if you could leave her out of all this."

"Thierry."

"See, she pretends I'm not half fae and, well, I let her. But you slapped her with a reminder."

"Thierry."

"What?"

"I don't know where your mother lives."

CHAPTER FIFTEEN

"I don't understand." Horns blared behind me as I cut off traffic. "Who sent Mom the Bird-O-Gram?"

My thoughts turned to the voice from the shower. He had warned me away from the Rook. Were the birds another warning? Or were they a threat? I didn't know, and I wasn't taking chances with Mom's life.

In the passenger seat, Raven braced his hands on the dash. His nails sank into the plastic and would leave crescent shapes behind.

"Enemies of Faerie," he gritted through a tight jaw.

I punched the horn, warning other drivers out of my way. "Vague much?"

"There are those who seek war after so many centuries of peace." He swallowed hard. "There are others who disagree with you being given a choice. They believe that, as the Black Dog's daughter, it is your duty to fulfil his obligations until he returns, even if you must be persuaded to cooperate."

Dread tightened my chest. "Persuaded how?"

When he didn't answer, my mind filled the blanks in horrific detail and my foot stomped on the accelerator.

"Why black birds?" I demanded.

"Crows and ravens are—" His sentence ended in snarled liquid syllables when his head bounced off the window after we skidded left.

"Death omens," I finished the thought for him.

"They are also evidence as incriminating as a fingerprint." His voice lowered. "Someone doesn't want you to trust me."

"Well, mission accomplished." I wish I had free hands to slow clap. "I don't trust you or anyone else with a Faerie agenda."

Raven grimaced. "When was the last time you saw your mother?"

I tallied the flipped-shifts I'd worked since then in my head. "Two days ago."

He didn't have anything to add.

I clenched my teeth. "If anything has happened to her..."

"I will accept responsibility."

"That's not good enough."

One more hard right made Raven flinch, and then we were there. Mom's house.

He yanked his fingers from their indents in the dash, leaned back and shut his eyes.

A whimper brought our attention to the backseat. The stink of ammonia lit up my nose. Great. Bad Luck Bunny had wet his furry britches. I almost felt sorry for him. Almost.

Raven's lip curled. "What about the púca?"

"Leave him." Sean was no longer a priority.

After throwing open the car door, I climbed out and ran up to the house. The front door stood ajar. The knob cracked against the wall when I shoved it out of my way and barreled inside. The TV was off, both the living room and the kitchen light dark.

"Do you see a car in the garage? The big room next door to the house?" I called to Raven, who stood on the welcome mat. He vanished, and I worked my way from room to room. "Mom?" I gulped down my panic. "Are you home?"

"I looked through the slats." Raven's voice rose behind me. "An orange car is in the large room."

"Mom gets carsick if she isn't driving. There's no way she left with anyone in theirs. That means she took her afternoon walk early or..." I swallowed hard, "...something has happened."

Shoving past Raven, I hit the hallway leading to her bedroom, flipping on lights as I went, popping my head into the rooms I hadn't checked yet. Empty. Dark. Empty. Dark. Her room was my last hope. I rested my hand on the knob, inhaled and pushed open the door. The glow from her plug-in air freshener cast a halo over her throw pillows. Resting atop one lilac-colored sham curled a single black feather.

Lifting my feet took more effort the nearer I got to her bed.

I pinched that feather between my fingers and turned to Raven. "What does this mean?"

He took it from me, his eyes narrowing. "Your mother has been taken."

"First the birds on her lawn and now this," I snarled. "Black birds and black feathers, *Raven*."

"I know how this looks," he said softly.

"It looks a hell of a lot like you're behind this." I shoved him against the wall and braced my forearm against his throat. "Tell me you didn't do this. Give me your word, as the Morrigan's son, or I'm dragging your ass in front of the magistrates right now."

His breathing remained calm. "I vow, as the Morrigan's son, I did not take your mother."

My arm went limp, and I backed away as it fell. "How do you know she was taken?"

"There are carvings in the shaft of the feather." He held it out to me. "They're runes. The same ones used to operate the tether between realms. They were leaving you a means of following them."

I snatched the feather and studied the foreign symbols. "They took her to Faerie."

I had screwed up. I should have gone to the magistrates immediately. I had been too slow making up my mind about Raven's offer, and now some asshat from Faerie had made it up for me.

I stormed through the house headed for my car. I tugged my cellphone from my pocket and sent Shaw a text to meet me at the office ASAP.

"Wait." Raven grabbed my arm and took the feather. "Where are you going?"

"To the magistrates." I shrugged him off me. "They're the only ones who can get her back."

He pocketed the blackened quill. "You overestimate the conclave's influence in Faerie."

"The magistrates are nobles." One Seelie and one Unseelie, as every conclave outpost required. "Are you saying Faerie won't listen to its own nobility?"

"Those who are sent to monitor this realm are outcast from their families." Raven corralled me against the car. "In the eyes of the High Court, this is all they are fit to do. The consuls in Faerie couldn't care less what magistrates here have to say. They are lesser nobles. Not benevolent ambassadors as you seem to believe."

"I'll have to take my chances." I shoved him stumbling back and slid into the driver's seat.

He caught the door before I slammed it. "I'm sorry, Thierry."

I glared up at him. "Sorry doesn't cut it."

"The conclave can't know I'm here." He squatted to put us at eye level. "No one can."

"I filed a report after you poached from the Morrigan." I stretched that statement into a lie. "They know you're responsible."

"That is unfortunate." He clamped a hand over my wrist. "That means your time is up."

"What are you talking about?" Tugging against him got me exactly nowhere.

"If the magistrates know I'm here, they will be watching the tethers." Urgency spiked his tone. "I can't risk being trapped in this realm."

He placed my hands on the wheel. Magic wound over my wrists and stuck my hands in place. He shut the door, circled the car and climbed onto the seat beside me.

I struggled against the invisible restraints. "What are you doing?"

"What I should have done in the first place." He grimaced. "I'm taking you home to Faerie."

Compelled by Raven's magic, I drove straight to the conclave, which suited me just fine. We sat in the parked car, him peering through his window and me praying Shaw was racing up the drive behind us. Raven pursed his lips and squinted his eyes. Call me crazy, but I got the impression the glamours applied to this place slid right off before his eyes. No Word required.

All I saw and all I would see until I deactivated the wards was the glamour depicting a dilapidated farmhouse and the adjacent field.

"You can't sneak past the guards." I grunted while tugging on my hands. "You're going to get caught."

"I don't think so." He studied a point in the distance. "I've already done this once, remember?"

"You separated your consciousness and crossed the ward in pieces." I looked him up and down. "You're fully formed now."

"It will require more finesse," he agreed. "For one thing, there are two of us."

I ground my teeth. "I'm not going to Faerie until I speak with the magistrates."

"You're trembling." He shifted toward me. "Are you frightened?"

"My mother was kidnapped, and according to you, she's being held hostage until I agree to be a temp for my father at court," I spat. "Of course I'm afraid."

"It's more than that." His intense gaze stripped me raw. "You're scared of the other side. Afraid of finding out how Faerie looks, what it's like there. Your mother poisoned you with her doubts. You fear cloaking yourself fully in the mantle of the Black Dog." His voice softened. "You have no idea what you truly are."

"Leave my mother out of this. She raised me. Macsen Sullivan was a sperm donor, not a parent."

Raven brushed a stray hair from my cheek. "This is the best chance you have to save your mother."

I snapped at his hand. "It just happens to also be the best chance you have of getting what you want."

He exited the car.

Think, Thierry. Escape seemed unlikely. Rescue was my best hope, but my knight in shining pickup truck was nowhere in sight.

Raven opened my door and bent inside. He passed his hands over mine, setting me free, and I leaned forward and bit his ear as hard as I could. Blood filled my mouth, and his curses spilled from the car. I shoved him backward and scrambled outside, hissing my Word and yanking off my glove. I took a step toward the marshal's office, but Raven tackled me.

Magic boiled in my fingertips when I clamped them around his wrist, but the power fizzled and dripped unspent to the ground. I pushed every ounce of energy I had into the hot runes where my bare palm touched his skin. Nada.

He clamped a hand over my mouth in anticipation of a scream I was too stunned to utter.

"We are both death portents," he panted. "We are immune to one another's magic."

I recovered enough to bite his palm until more of his blood coated my tongue.

Raven hissed an incantation, and my lips smashed together as if an invisible hand had stitched my mouth shut.

"You, however, are not immune to spells." He spun me toward him and gripped my upper arm. "I came prepared in the event you were uncooperative." He dragged me back to the car and patted me down. He found the phone and tossed it onto the seat. "You won't need that where we're going."

Another burst of magic hit the air as a second spell glued my feet to the ground.

"Don't worry about the púca." Raven circled the car, cracking the windows. "He has all he needs to survive until he's found." When Raven returned, his touch unstuck me. "I regret things had to be this way. I wanted to be your friend."

Some of my mumbled threats must have gotten through, because he scowled.

Friend? Not likely. This nonconsensual road trip into Faerie had put him squarely into enemy territory.

His quiet sigh might have conveyed remorse, but his slender fingers seemed less sympathetic as they dug into my upper arm. I struggled against him. He didn't bother noticing. He kept on walking.

Raven was escorting me to Faerie, even if I snarled and snapped at him every step of the way.

CHAPTER SIXTEEN

When Raven said he came prepared, he meant it. He conjured a pan flute and rested the top edge against his bottom lip. The flute was crafted from seven cuts of a hollow reed, dried and polished to a high shine, then lashed together with brown leather. Each segment was longer than the one before it. He held it by the shortest pipe and blew.

The glamour wrapping our surroundings rustled, tearing free and flapping on the magical breeze.

I leapt back and landed on my butt when chain link appeared to thrust from the ground not a foot from the toe of my shoe. My eyes bulged while the tattered glamour ripped from its frame and the prison exploded into full view.

The shreds of concealing magic drifted through the air in our direction. I worked my jaw to ask a question, realized I could open my mouth and figured the unbinding spell he played must be loosening the spells he had cast on me. I worked my stiff lips. "Wush happening?"

He didn't answer, but he did help me stand.

His music continued to shred the conclave's defenses while we stood exposed to anyone glancing our way. Over our heads, those ragged scraps of glamour gained speed. The first opaque flake smacked into me and stuck like tissue paper dipped in Mod Podge.

Raven's playing orchestrated a whirl of magical decoupage until I was covered from head to toe. A quick glance confirmed he was similarly plastered by magical debris. He lowered the pipe and, with a twist of his wrist, sent it back wherever he had conjured it from in the first place.

"Camouflage," he answered breathlessly. "Come on. The effect doesn't last long."

This time when he tugged, I resisted, but the spell on my feet was stronger than the one on my mouth, and I went where he led me, cursing all the while.

Beyond the prison, he urged me into a run, and I discovered his flute hadn't torn glamour from all of the buildings, only the ones nearest us. In the distance, I saw the field of withered corn, the skeletal stalks hunched and broken.

Our destination was a no-brainer. The old windmill. The tether to Faerie.

I figured we had arrived when Raven pulled up short in front of me, jerking me to a halt while he examined each of the structure's spindly legs. Or I assumed that's what he was doing based on how he started squinting into thin air and moving his lips. The area was off-limits to most personnel, including me, and I wished I could see what he was doing. Activating the tether into Faerie, yes, but how? That information would come in handy, especially since he had taken the feather with its coordinates. Say if I managed to escape, which I'll admit was becoming less likely by the minute.

Concentration lined Raven's face. Reaching toward nothing, he completed a complex ritual with the hand not anchoring me to the spot. His gaze drifted skyward as a gust of air blasted hairs into my eyes. What he saw up there brought a fierce grin to his face, which I immediately regretted admiring. He caught me at it, cranked his smile up several megawatts and drew me flush against him. His arms encircled my waist, his face dipped toward mine. "The first time is always the worst."

"What a guy thing to say." I managed to work my hands between us and shoved to give myself an inch of personal space.

"I envy you." Wild joy animated him. "You will see Faerie through fresh eyes as I never have."

A tiny ripple of fear collided with the doubt making my stomach churn.

"I want a guarantee," I blurted. "Promise no matter what happens to me, you will bring Mom home safely."

Raven's lips parted. "You have my word. Regardless of the outcome, I swear to you I will escort your mother safely to this realm." His gaze flicked upward. "That is the best bargain I can make."

Considering he had offered without first ensuring reciprocation from me, I nodded. "I accept."

One hand gripped my nape and guided my head onto his shoulder. The other wound around my waist in back, mashing my soft chest into his much firmer one. He cradled me against the coming storm as much as he was able. His lips moved in a chant at my ear while the world upended.

Three heartbeats passed in silence so loud my head ached. Too bright. My eyes watered. Air sat lighter in my lungs. I gasped until I coughed. Still panicked. Suffocating. Not enough oxygen. It hurt. Breathing hurt. Looking hurt. My skin hurt. Agony like each death I had ever dealt scoured me.

"Thierry?"

Strong hands gripped my shoulders, bruising my tender skin. I screamed until they vanished and my kneecaps sank into spongy ground. I leaned forward, bracing my palms on what felt like moss or peat. After a few minutes passed and I didn't die, I risked cracking open my eyelids. "This can't be real."

Color assaulted my eyes, taunting me with vibrant perfection. My brain tried matching names to shades and failed. Their sharp flavors sat on the tip of my tongue. I was tasting color? Wait… What?

The tether had dumped us into a lush meadow interrupted by gnarly trees covered in moss that sat up and blinked at us with tiny googly eyes that whirled. Mushrooms with jewel-toned caps stopped their steady procession up the side of the nearest trunk to examine us through pinprick eyes. A gorgeous turquoise butterfly fluttered past, only to be shot through the trachea by a toothpick-sized arrow fired from an equally miniature bow held by one of the mushrooms. With his hands. Because mushrooms totally had appendages. And eyes. And sharpshooter aim.

I'm losing my mind.

I plopped down onto my butt. "None of this makes sense."

Raven knelt beside me. "Faerie is sensation." He gripped my shoulder when I listed to one side. "Imagine a stamp and an ink pad. Faerie is the ink pad. Fae are the stamp. When you press the stamp into the ink, you saturate that being with magic. As you press the stamp to paper, each imprint, every new world or new creature, becomes more faded. Every pass holds less ink, less magic. Humans and the mortal realm are the third or fourth impression. There was little magic left by that point. For that reason, few humans have magic and their world—colors, tastes, sounds—are bland by comparison."

Third or fourth? Was he implying there were more realms than fae and mortal?

"Is this our savior?" a mocking voice carried on a fetid breeze.

Savior? Lifting my head required absolute concentration. "Who are you?"

Raven placed his hand on my shoulder. "Forgive her, Consul."

The voice sounded closer. "Has she been educated?"

My hackles rose. "I've been trained by the best marshals at the Southwestern Conclave."

Raven's grip on me tightened. "She is worthy to bear Macsen's legacy."

I raked a measuring glance over him. How long had he observed me before making contact? A while if he had claimed three of the Morrigan's tithes to sustain him before mine. And closely, since he threw his weight behind my endorsement.

The consul's dismissive attitude grated on me, but I held my tongue. While in this realm, I was at their mercy. With my father missing, I had no one to trust. No one other than the High Court to appeal to, and the idea of conferring with them left me quaking in my sneakers.

"Escort her to the Halls of Winter." A soft chuckle. "My counterpart and I await you there."

Raven gave a curt nod to thin air. He stared at the spot in the trees where the voice had originated.

What kept me from drilling him for answers, I couldn't say. Curious as I was, instinct warned me to keep silent.

"Come with me," he whispered near my ear. "We will be safer in Winter. There are fewer eyes there."

The Halls, where he, as a prince, lived. Every step brought me deeper into his world.

When he rose and offered me his hand, I didn't hesitate. I took it, hoping this wasn't the second biggest mistake I had ever made by extending him even this much trust when he had done nothing to earn it. The first being when I fell for his sneaky ploy and rode the elevator up to investigate his apartment.

The spot where we had landed caught my eye. Mom had been cast into this world, disoriented and alone, no one holding her or reassuring her. Macsen was her only ally in Faerie, and who knew where he had gone? For now the path of least resistance made the most tactical sense, so I did as Raven asked.

Thanks, Dad.

Nineteen years ago, I was the mess he left behind. Now here I was, cleaning up after him.

CHAPTER SEVENTEEN

We kept to the lush forests, hidden among the vibrant foliage, skirting the twisted roads and avoiding the quaint towns that were welcome civilization amid the sprawling wilderness of the fae realm.

Foreign scents pummeled my nose until my sense of smell grew numb. I toddled after Raven as a drowsy child trailed after a parent, trusting him to guide me while I acclimated to this bizarre paint-by-numbers world.

Here plants sang. Birds sprouted flowers from their crests. Even trees met your gaze through lichen-encrusted lashes. My brain spluttered while absorbing it all.

"I would have prepared you better if I had known how strong your reaction would be."

Tearing my gaze from the sight of a prim white mouse wearing a kilt and wedge-shaped hat with trailing ribbons, carrying a miniature set of highland bagpipes, I zeroed in on Raven.

Words from his mouth intoxicated me as if I had drunk them.

As my ears learned how to filter out the white noise of Faerie, the butterfly giggles and ambient music heavy in the air, I strained against the melodiousness of Raven's voice above all the other enticements.

I tilted my head. "Do you sound how chocolate-covered strawberries taste because you're a prince?"

Pale as his skin was, the pink rising in his cheeks gave him a rosy glow.

"No." He glanced away. "I sound—"

"—edible—"

"—because you're intoxicated."

I blinked at him. "How is that possible?"

The edges of his eyes crinkled. "Those toadstools you were talking to earlier?"

"They said *hello*." Their voices like ants on helium. "It would have been rude to ignore them."

A full-on smile curved his lips. "They release hallucinogenic spores into the air."

"Wait." I pulled on his arm. "Then how do you know anything in Faerie is real?"

"There are no toadstools in the cities, and you build up a tolerance," he assured me. "I witnessed a human cycle through the process a long time ago. Since you are half fae, you will transition faster."

"Speaking of humans…" I kept my voice level. "How will Mom handle the transition?"

"At worst, she will be disoriented for a few days." He swatted at a tiny pest by his ear. "At best, her captors planned ahead and brought provisions to ease her acclimation. Given her status, it would be in their best interest to keep her comfortable. You would be disinclined to negotiate with them otherwise."

He took my hand and led me underneath mossy tree limbs wreathed with thorny vines. A sharp sting at my earlobe wrung a curse out of me. Figuring a thorn was to blame, I flinched when I reached up and felt something the size of a half dollar stuck to my ear. *Please, please, please don't be a tick.* The harder I tugged, the tighter it clung.

"Beware," a small voice chimed. "Beware the Rook. Beware the Rook. You are his pawn."

The cold fingers of déjà vu caressed my spine.

One hard yank and the not-a-tick came off in my hand. Its tiny face was streaked with reddish-brown stripes like war paint, and its fangs were flashing. It bit my thumb and drew blood.

It was an actual pixie, like the ones from the children's books Mom never read to me.

Two inches tall at the most, it was beautifully androgynous and—*ouch*—a little bastard.

I tightened my grip before holding it closer to my face. "What did you say?"

It clamped its hands over its pointed ears and screeched.

Holding it at arm's length, I whispered, "Sorry."

"Thierry?" Raven stared at my hand. "What is that?"

"It's a pixie." I twisted my hand for his inspection. "It bit me."

"They do that." He glanced between it and me. "Did it say anything?"

The pixie's eyes grew round. It shivered in my fist despite the balmy warmth.

It was scared. No. Terrified. Of Raven.

Hot liquid puddled in my palm and dripped through my fingers. Great. Peed on by a pixie. Now my adventure was complete.

"Oh yuck." I used that as an excuse to fling the tiny fae from my hand. It fluttered its wings, trailing glittering light as it zoomed into the canopy overhead. "Should it have?"

He tore a papery leaf from a nearby tree and passed it to me. "They sometimes act as messengers."

"Oh really?" I paid close attention to drying my hand to keep from meeting his gaze.

"Remember that pixies are small-minded creatures," he said. "They often confuse messages."

If I hadn't heard that same threat before, then I might be more willing to believe him.

But I had, and I wasn't.

Raven was the one person who could tell me who the Rook was and what danger he posed to me, but the stark fear in that pixie's eyes when he spotted Raven made me hesitant to ask. Someone had gone to great lengths to warn me away from Raven, but who? A Seelie rival of his? Or someone else, someone eager for the war Raven mentioned?

Confrontation was out of the question. I needed Raven to get me to the Halls where I could meet with fae who could help Mom. What I didn't need was for him to get his feathers in a twist and leave me out here on my own. As easily as Faerie had enchanted me, I would be licking rocks or carousing with toads before nightfall.

The smart thing would be to bribe Mable into making discreet inquiries about Rook after I got home.

"I'll keep that in mind." I let the damp leaf flutter to the ground. "How much farther?"

"Another mile." He started walking. "Maybe two."

Behind his back, I scanned the air for my winged messenger. It was gone. Unscathed I hoped.

I jogged a few steps to catch him. "Will someone be at the Halls I can ask about Mom?"

"Yes." He picked up his pace. "You will have your answers when we arrive."

"That guy, the consul." Yet another fae who preferred the disembodied-voice approach to conversation. "Who is he?"

"It's not safe to talk here. When we reach the Halls, all your questions will be answered. Trust me for a while longer." He glanced over his shoulder. "You will…hear things about me there."

"Let me guess." I chuckled. "I shouldn't believe them because they aren't true?"

When our gazes met, something old and tired drifted behind his eyes.

"Believe the worst of me," he said at last, "and I will never disappoint you."

"Lucky you, I come standard with daddy issues. I don't trust easily." I couldn't afford to in my line of work. "That goes double for fae men."

"Even Shaw?" he asked softly.

Frowning at Raven's back, wondering how much he knew about us, I told him the absolute truth. "Especially Shaw."

I almost froze to death before we reached the Halls of Winter.

Twelve steps outside of the jungle, the sheet of mirror-smooth ice had started. A moat he said. Skating across had been fun. The humid breath of the forest interior still curled over the ice to warm me. I even laughed.

I was an idiot.

The solid moat led to a castle built from colossal blocks of ice, mortared together with snow. I screamed on the first step onto the snowbank surrounding the fortress. Tears froze in my eyes. Their glassy shine distorted my view of what came next. An ornate door to one side of the structure swung open when we reached it. Hard to tell for sure, but I saw no one responsible for our welcome.

Inside was bliss. I collapsed in a heap before Raven caught me. I shoved him away and sat there, soaking in the warmth of the room's blazing fire as my skin thawed. I reached an icy hand toward its beckoning heat but was too exhausted to walk the requisite steps to sit in the chair before the hearth.

Rather than argue or manhandle me, Raven snapped his fingers.

The fire stood up on flame-kissed legs and walked to me, leaving sooty footprints in its wake.

"T-t-thanks." I stretched my fingers and let my joints thaw. "F-f-fire elem-m-mental?"

"He is." Raven left me on the opaque tile floor and crossed to the chair, which he angled toward me before he sat. "He's been with our family for centuries."

Footsteps rang out behind me. I was too weary to check who they belonged to.

"Shall I warm some broth for the *Cú Sídhe*?" a cultured voice asked. "Or for you, my lord?"

"Thierry, are you hungry?" Raven rose and crossed the room to a cabinet, where he poured three fingers of amber liquid in a squat glass that resembled the iced block walls. "Drink this. It will help."

I accepted the drink, swirling the contents. "What is it?"

"Single malt whiskey." He took the glass from me and sipped. "It's not poisoned or spelled."

I stuck out my hand, trusting he wouldn't kill me or let me die before he got what he wanted.

The first swallow lit my throat on fire. The next sent my chest up in flames. The third ignited in my stomach and the fourth simmered the numbness from my limbs. A fifth would have rendered me to glowing embers. Good thing Raven pried the glass from my hand and polished off the amber dregs.

A throat cleared behind me. I was thawed enough to turn this time.

"Whoa." I covered my mouth. "Please tell me I didn't say that out loud."

The servant didn't smile, but amusement thawed the chill in his eyes.

He was tall and lean—definitely sidhe—but was as colorless as the heart of winter. His skin was as pale as Raven's, his outline limned in faint silver light. His irises were ivory. Even his hair, the same length as his master's, was snow white with silver strands threading the queue down his spine.

"I set two places in the dining hall." He bowed to Raven. "I will serve, if it pleases you."

"Leave the tureen. We can serve ourselves." Raven extended his hand and pulled me onto my feet. He eased into my line of sight, forcing my attention onto him. "Bháin, you are dismissed."

I peered around Raven's shoulder. "What is he, if it's not rude to ask?"

"He is a servant of winter." Raven grasped my elbow. "His kind seeded the lore for Jack Frost."

"That is amazing." My part of Texas didn't see snow often, which explained why I experienced wonder when those rare flakes fell instead of swearing when forced to procure a shovel or a bag of rock salt.

Raven steered me down a long hallway lit with peculiar spheres of light. "I suppose."

Portraits decorated the hall. The décor could be summed up in one word: macabre.

Battle scenes raged across the walls. Weapons hung on pegs, proud of the carnage they had wrought. Stylized black birds flew on a coat of arms adorning shields and helmets interspersed among the art.

Yes, it was fitting, but non-death related pursuits were nice too. In fact, I much preferred them. The human in me must be spoiling my gore-loving death dealer heritage.

I valued life. I mourned its loss. I carried the guilt of every life I ended, and I never forgot my victims' faces.

Unnerved by the silence, I said the first thing that came to mind. "Nice portraits."

He glanced around as though he had forgotten they were there. "Mother commissioned them."

That didn't surprise me. "Is the macabre not your thing?"

He shrugged. "I avoid introspection if that's what you're asking."

I did too, and our ages were no comparison. "So the art bothers you?"

"To admit I am disturbed by the art is to admit I am disturbed by my life." He paused outside a slender archway. "Despite what you may think, your father did a service to you by allowing your mother to raise you. He would have been called home eventually and brought you with him. The fae realm is no place to raise a half-blood child, and even if he wished your mother to come with him, that favor would have been denied. You would have grown up without her, without your humanity."

"If he stayed, innocent lives would have been saved." I walked past Raven. "He could have taught me how to deal with a talent I still don't understand." When I spotted the dining table, I had to grin. "This is right out of a cartoon."

Each side must have held fifty place settings. If I squinted, I could just make out the foot of the table. The tureen Raven had mentioned sat near the head of the table. A place was set there and before the chair to its right. I sensed there was significance attached to our seating arrangement I was missing, but the trek through Faerie had depleted me. All I had left was enough strength to stubbornly hold out for assurances from Raven that what I was about to eat wasn't going to further obligate me to him somehow.

He positioned himself behind the chair to the right of where he must always sit and pulled it out for me.

"Before you deprive yourself of a meal, let me assure you what you eat here is freely given. The food is payment for your troubles. There are no bindings, spells, charms or hexes attached." His tone held amusement. "We will dine here, replenish ourselves and then continue on to the Halls of Winter."

I gestured around the room. "This isn't the Halls of Winter?"

"This is my private residence." He indicated the waiting chair. "Please, sit."

"Not until you explain why we made a detour. Is this where your contact man is meeting us?"

"No." He sighed. "Those matters will be discussed at the Halls."

I scowled at him. "Then why are we wasting time here?"

"You're tired and hungry. You need to be sharp when you meet the High Court consuls."

I blasted out an exhale and sank into the chair. He had a point.

A Seelie King might sit upon the throne, but the Faerie High Court was the highest collective power in the land. Since Mac was one of three cabinet members, if anyone could help me, it was them.

"Their sole interest in meeting with you is to discuss the matter of your father's disappearance. Under the circumstances, you can use their desperation to your advantage. You must bargain with them for the safe return of your mother and for passage home."

"I wouldn't have made it this far without you." I folded my hands in my lap. "So...thanks."

"Be careful who you thank, Thierry." He froze in place. "Some would see it as a favor owed."

"Damn. That's Fae 101." I rubbed my face. "It just slipped out."

"You're exhausted, and you're still transitioning." He opened the tureen and ladled a dark brown broth into my bowl that smelled of marrow, garlic and onions. "That is why you are going to eat first, rest and prepare yourself to face them."

Gratitude welled in me as I lifted my spoon and ran it around the bowl, stirring the mixture and inhaling the rich scent. "It's kind of you to be so considerate." Though I didn't doubt there was a cost to his goodwill.

His soft chuckles brought a twinkle to his eyes. "It is my pleasure to serve you."

I lifted a spoonful to my mouth and tried to be discreet when I inhaled. It smelled clean, no magic, poisons or other familiar dangers, and the whiff of mouthwatering fragrance perked up my stomach. The brown color made me think of beef. Living in Texas, well, everything made me think of beef. But there weren't any cows in Faerie.

Instead of asking what sort of creature donated its bones to the pot, I waited for Raven to serve himself. Once he joined me at the table, I tucked into my meal.

The faint smile Raven wore as he ate concerned me, but not enough to bother asking him a question when I figured he would tap dance around the answer. Though I would have preferred some conversation to drown out the scraping of our spoons on porcelain, I wasted no time talking that could be spent eating. The faster I emptied my bowl, the quicker we left and the closer I came to going home.

CHAPTER EIGHTEEN

My toes were tapping while I waited for Raven to finish his meal. When Bháin entered the room with a leather-wrapped parcel in his arms, I figured it must have been a delivery made while the lord of the manor was in the mortal realm. My surprise was genuine when he brought it to me instead.

"A gift from the master." Bháin extended his arms so I could do the honors. "It won't bite."

This time the throat cleared was Raven's.

Bháin lowered his head. "Forgive my familiarity, lady."

"You're fine." I recoiled from the parcel. "I can't accept that, whatever it is."

"You must if you're going to survive the rest of the journey." Raven pushed to his feet and came to my side. He murmured in Bháin's ear and then relieved him of the package. "You are dismissed."

His response chimed like thousands of crystal glasses toasting the beauty of the sidhe language.

Raven's expression darkened, and he responded in kind, his tone shattering the fragile beauty of the previous comments, a hammer that smashed those crystalline words into ragged shards.

Fascination tuned me in deeper to their conversation than was polite, but I lacked the facilities to understand their language, let alone speak it.

Raven raised his hand in Bháin's face. "Enough. Your point has been made."

Trying to affect a casual air before they deigned to notice me again, I faced straight forward and examined the frosted wall opposite me. Good thing I had glossed over its bleak portrait grouping before I ate.

I wasn't much for beheadings.

Bháin cleared my place and then the rest of the table without uttering another sound. He finished and left me in the hall alone with Raven, who clutched the bundle to his chest while unlacing the ties.

"Be careful who you give your trust." He snapped a knotted cord. "Even the guileless carry swords here."

"I am being careful." The broth had done wonders for clearing my head. "I appreciate what you have done for me so far, but I can't accept a gift from you without further obligating myself."

He dropped the bundle onto the table in front of me. "It's your choice. Live to negotiate for your mother's safe return. Or die before we reach the Halls of Winter and leave her at her captors' mercy."

"What you're saying is I have no choice." I toyed with the wrapping. "No surprise given how I came to be here."

Well and truly stuck, I opened the parcel. "Is that armor?"

I lifted the topmost piece, a molded-leather breastplate I bet a month's salary would hug all my curves. How those curves had been measured, I wasn't sure I wanted to know. A black shirt was under that. A pair of pants covered in lightweight scales sat on the bottom of the stack. No. I was wrong. Socks were in there too. What worried me most was the outfit reeked of magic…and elves. Not that it was wholly unexpected. Children's stories limited elves' creativity to footwear, but they crafted whatever struck their fancy. Armor included.

Those stories had been exaggerated in other ways too. Some fae were content to work for honey or other relatively inexpensive or common items. Cobbling elves weren't one of them, and whoever went through the trouble of making and enchanting this outfit… They were walking around several gold bars lighter.

Raven caressed my cheek. "Try it on."

"No." I shoved the mound of clothing aside. "It's too much. I can't accept it."

His other hand rose to smooth his forehead. "You are picking the wrong battles."

"I'm protecting myself the best way I know how." No gifts. No thanks. No perceived debts.

"Fine." He scooped up the pile and strode down the hall.

I lasted all of five seconds before I leapt to my feet and followed. "What are you doing?"

"These were made for you." He reached the door, opened it and flung them onto the icy ground. "You don't want them, and no one else can trigger their magic. I have no reason for keeping them."

I gaped at the senseless waste. "Those must have cost you a fortune."

"I have resources." He shrugged. "The cost was not an issue."

Right. Princes must inherit small fortunes along with the title.

Waving a hand at him, I shooed him aside. "Get out of the way."

He stepped to the left and unlatched the lock I hadn't seen him trigger.

I opened the door and scowled at the heap of clothing smudging the winter-white landscape. Darting outside, I gathered the scattered outfit and ran back in to melt the snow stuck in my hair.

I dumped it all in a heap on the floor then returned to the hearth and the crackling fire elemental. It flared brighter at my approach, which earned it a smile, then flamed hotter to thaw my icy fingers.

"I knew you couldn't resist." The smugness in Raven's voice was thicker than the honey I gifted Mable.

"Not everyone was born with a silver spoon in their mouth. Some of us work for a living." The cost of that outfit would have paid my rent for five years. "So no, I couldn't leave the clothes to ruin."

Raven shoved off the wall where he had been leaning. "Your father doesn't provide for you?"

"Not a penny." I massaged the stinging from my hands. "I pay my own way."

He cocked his head. "I didn't realize."

"That I wasn't a kept woman?" I scoffed. "Sorry to disillusion you."

He sounded thoughtful. "I would have handled this situation differently if I had known."

"The ratty couch wasn't your first clue?" I laughed. "Or the rattletrap car I drive?"

His brows slanted downward. "They were low quality, but you seemed pleased with them."

"I am pleased with them." Heat stung my neck until I rubbed it. "Let's just—new topic okay?"

Finally I understood why talking money was considered crass at worst, borderline rude at best.

For those who never worried where their next meal was coming from, fear of going hungry was as foreign as my first step into Faerie.

A throat clearing brought my attention back to Raven.

"No time. We have to leave." He gestured toward the clothes. "You must dress quickly."

I straightened from the fire, mourning the loss of its heat. "I'm not accepting your gift."

"What gift? Do you mean those clothes you found discarded on my property? Those aren't mine. Not my size." He canted his head. "It's your choice. Use them or not."

"You are..." I rolled a few choice words around my head before settling on, "...sneaky."

A tight smile stretched his lips. "I have been called worse."

I just bet he had.

Even after being assured I was under no obligation to accept or wear the gift Raven had offered, I couldn't make myself do either. What frightened me was not being given freedom to choose, but fear of making the wrong choice. I had never intended to visit Faerie, and I wasn't prepared for it.

Basic fae etiquette had been drummed into my head, but I had never bargained with a creature like this.

Raven could destroy me. He could twist any one of the missteps I had made around him until he owned me. That he hadn't yet didn't mean he wouldn't ever. It just meant I was of more use to him running on my own steam, making fresh mistakes to compound the old ones than under his auspices.

When he excused himself to freshen up, my fingers began itching to fling the pile of armor into the fire. That was one way to make a decision, right? His return made me grateful I had resisted the temptation.

Gone were the trappings of the mortal realm. Raven wore a black leather outfit, one part armor and two parts fashion plate, that complemented the one he'd had made for me. Silver-studded gloves stretched to his elbows. His shoulders were masked by epaulets fashioned from sleek black feathers of varying lengths and a heavy cloak fastened underneath. Free of its braid, his hair hung dark and smooth down his back.

The slight peak at his forehead was accentuated by the elegant sterling circlet he wore. An oversight maybe, since he dressed quickly, but the crest in its center was inverted. The stylized bird with a serpent clutched in its talons flew upside down. I was about to draw his attention to it but decided against it.

Care had been taken with every aspect of his appearance. Not one hair on his head was out of place. He chose to wear his crown upside down. Why? If it was a political statement, I was better off ignorant. I gladly fisted my thin plausible deniability in a chokehold and kept my questions to myself.

Taking all this into consideration, I made the best decision with the information available.

I forced out the words. "Is there somewhere I can change?"

A pleased gleam lit his eyes, but I let it pass without comment. Silent in his triumph, he gathered the clothes and escorted me to an enormous bedroom decorated in the same requisite shades of black as the rest of the house. I squinted to make out ornate details because of the monochromatic scheme.

Jeans and a faded denim shirt covered the arm of a black damask chair by the cold hearth.

Hello, master suite.

Why not? I mean, in a residence this size, empty rooms must be *so* difficult to come by.

He set my clothes on the bed, *his* bed, sorting the individual pieces as if concerned I might skip one then pointed toward the far right corner. "The bath is there if you want to refresh yourself before you change."

"I might take you up on that." I was grimy, and I wanted to make a good impression.

That desire to impress had been what tipped the scales in his favor.

The consuls would look at me and measure me against my father. I wouldn't stack up. I knew it. Right now I looked human, and fae didn't esteem mortals. I needed their respect if I wanted them to bargain with me fairly. I had one way to get it, assuming all royal fae weren't immune to my talent the way Raven was, but going that route meant someone had to die needlessly in order for me to make my point.

If clothes made the fae, then it was time I dressed the part.

CHAPTER NINETEEN

Constant tickling on my throat finally made me snap. My fashion statement might have suffered, but I yanked four tail feathers from the mini epaulets attached to the leather straps on my breastplate.

Raven cut his eyes in my direction.

I pretended not to notice.

We had left his home what felt like hours ago. Though my outfit was thin, the heat-spelled lining kept me toasty. The worst damage I took trudging through the powdery snow on Raven's heels was cracked lips and a wind-burned face. My cheeks must have glowed red and raw as much as they stung. His remained pale and smooth as always.

The farther we trekked, the more relaxed he appeared and the tenser I became. We traveled deep into the heart of his house's holdings. The tingling in my scalp told me this was not a place I should ever have seen.

Faerie was divided into seasons that mirrored the mortal realm, except all four seasons coexisted here. This world wasn't spherical like Earth. Faerie was more of a geographic map, and it was possible to fall off the edges. Though it was more likely you would be eaten before that happened.

Winter, with its darkly creeping longer nights, belonged to Unseelie House. Summer, with its brightly languorous days, belonged to Seelie House. Autumn and Spring were neutral ground, but Mable told me once that Autumn was in Winter's pocket and Spring had ties to Summer. Considering their seasonal segregations, it seemed odd the Halls of Winter would handle negotiations, unless that was an admission of guilt in itself. Still, shouldn't we head toward Autumn? It favored Unseelie, which ought to put Raven at ease, without alienating the Seelie.

The way I saw it, I was a neutral party. Autumn was neutral ground. Neutrality was what I needed in order to avoid being seen as having a preference for either side.

Arriving dressed to match with a dark fae prince to the Halls of Winter made a statement.

Freaking fae men and their games. Mom had been right to warn me about them.

"Look there." Raven's voice carried over the wind. "The Halls of Winter."

I followed his line of sight to a fortress made of ice blocks, each rectangular brick taller than I was. Turrets rose in three of the four corners. In the farthest corner, an enormous platform hung suspended over a quarter of the exposed interior courtyard.

Snow hung dense in the air. Fat clouds covered the upper portions of the structure, obscuring it from view. What puzzled me most were the guards walking along the walls. Each held a black cable that stretched into the clouds. For all I knew, another tier of rooms were concealed high over their heads and those thick ropes hung from a... No. That couldn't be right.

The men walked. The ropes moved with them. Not stationary so... "What am I looking at?"

Raven's chuckle heated my ear. "You will see."

Though I should have known better, the glint of mischief in his eyes heightened my anticipation.

What was I about to see? How was he so certain it would blow my mind?

Better yet, why did he care what I thought?

We crested a small hill and were met by an honest-to-God ogre. He was taller than most trees, and the ground rumbled under our feet as the creature's lips moved. Boulders collided in his voice. His grumbled words sounded foreign to my ears, and they were beyond my comprehension.

Raven answered him in that grating language then lifted his hand, and a pulse of black magic whirled across his palm.

With a tight nod of acknowledgement, the ogre fell to its knees before him, knocking me onto my ass in the snow.

Raven hooked his arm under mine. "He won't harm you on purpose, but stay on your guard. Accidents with ogres can prove fatal."

My shoulders stiffened. Was he implying accidentally on purpose?

Maybe the ogre didn't like playing gatekeeper. Or maybe he just didn't like half-bloods like me.

I leaned against Raven. "I'll keep that in mind."

He glanced down at me. "Hold on."

"Why should I…?"

The ogre speared his fingers into the ground before us, shoveling the frozen chunk of dirt where we stood into his palm and lifting us to his shoulder height before his eye caught mine and he grinned.

My knees turned to rubber. Let him laugh. It would serve him right if I puked on his knuckles.

A strong arm circled my waist—Raven's—and held me tight against his side. "You'll be fine."

"As long as I don't look down?" I covered my mouth before I emptied my stomach.

"We're almost there." His thumb tapped my hip absently. "It will be worthwhile. I promise."

I elbowed his hand. "You're half bird, of course you aren't scared."

His lips were back at my ear, his breath hot on my throat. "I won't let you fall."

Terrified of testing his promise, I didn't punch him again. Oh, but I wanted to.

I crushed my eyes closed and focused on breathing while the ogre hummed a tune and the world trembled in our passage. I had almost succeeded in convincing myself I wasn't going to be eaten or flung to my death when the ride stopped and the hand beneath us began moving, threatening to topple me.

Raven squeezed my shoulder. "Look now."

The cables were a few hundred yards away, and we stood higher than the guards' heads. I let my gaze travel the length of one strand from a youthful fae's hand up into the clouds and...my knees gave.

I knelt on a clod of dirt clutched in an ogre's hand, and I stared up at the impossible.

My voice cracked. "Those are dragons."

Raven stared up at them, wonder absent in his gaze. "They are."

"Those don't exist," I explained to him very slowly. "Not even in Faerie."

In search of richer nesting grounds, dragons had followed the first fae into the mortal realm where they were hunted to extinction by humans. All the history books said so. Yet there they were. Breathing. Flying. *Alive*.

The sleek lizards gliding over my head wore glistening metallic scales, and there were two beasts for each primary color. Their tails were streamers sailing in their wake. With serpentine necks, their heads were the size of entire horses with teeth the length of my arm. Wings extended from either side of their spines on nubby arms. Between finger-like striations, the skin looked as thin as silk.

Each wore a thick leather bridle clasped with a black cable.

"Mother has an affinity for winged creatures." Raven swept out his arm. "This is her legacy."

The edge of bitterness made me seek his face. "Not her son?"

"Heirs die." His eyes hardened. "Bastards rise." He glanced at me. "Legends are immortal."

"How does no one know this?" A legend was only as effective as its reach.

"The Unseelie know, when it is important they should remember." He made it sound like that was enough. "There is an enchantment on the beasts. Anyone may see them while on these grounds. Unless the visitor has been given the gift of recall, they forget the dragons after they leave, thus protecting their existence."

I soaked in their ethereal beauty. "I will forget them."

"For now." His gaze went distant. "There is always later to consider."

As the ogre's hand swung past the landing pad, Raven asked, "Would you like a closer look?"

"No." I turned my back on them. "That's not why I'm here. I can't play tourist with you."

"Another time perhaps." He called out to the ogre, "To the front gate."

Gravity ceased to exist. The ogre lowered his hand so fast my feet left the ground, hair flew over my head. With sweaty palms, I clutched Raven's arm. Unflustered by the free fall, he was my anchor.

Before the ogre's knuckles brushed the pavers leading to the main gate, he slowed our descent. My knees buckled, and I sat down hard. He twisted his wrist and dropped us—dirt clod and all—onto the path. Still on my knees, I leaned forward on my hands and kissed the icy ground. While my churning gut settled, I braced my spinning forehead against the cold stones under my palms.

Raven took my arm and forced me to my feet. "It's dangerous to show weakness here."

I broke his grip. "I'm about to show what I had for lunch."

"That would be unwise."

"As unwise as wandering around this place with you?"

His face cracked into a smile. "As guides go, you could do worse."

That circlet must be on too tight. This wasn't a sightseeing tour or a vacation. This was a rescue mission. At least, that's what I kept telling myself to stop dwelling on the part where I hadn't exactly came here willingly either. Raven was the means through which my goals would be achieved.

Once the ink dried on the deals we were about to make, he would be my ticket home.

"We should get inside." I stepped toward the door. "I don't want to keep them waiting."

Raven's strides matched mine as we met the guards and gained entry. We were led through long halls that called Raven's home to mind. Ornate fireplaces acted as centerpieces in every room we passed, warming the air to a bearable degree. Their fires lacked the friendly warmth of Raven's. The dripping mantles and puddled hearths convinced me the fires were coaxed from wood and elbow grease, not the product of elemental magic.

More's the pity. It was handy having a fire come when you called it.

"Wait here." He eased in front of me. "I don't want there to be any surprises."

I nodded and stepped to one side.

When the door opened before us, he ducked inside a dimly lit room that smelled of rich incense. Myrrh undertones made my nasal passages itch.

Grateful for a moment alone, I straightened my clothing and smoothed my windblown hair with trembling fingers. I shoved all thoughts of dragons and ogres and elementals into the back of my mind.

When Raven returned, I was ready. One look at his formidable expression made me hesitate.

What had he gotten me into?

CHAPTER TWENTY

Potent magic slithered over me, making my skin crawl as I entered the gloomy chamber. The enormous room was empty. Nothing decorated the space except for the massive tapestries depicting winter scenes. Straight ahead of us, built into the ice-block wall, was a low balcony. Two identical mirrors, both longer than I was tall, were tacked onto the wall behind the railing, and two matching chairs sat before them.

A path lined with flickering candles led us through the shadowy expanse to a small circle scraped into the frozen floor. Raven stepped inside it without hesitation. I did not. Circles were common symbols used by witches and other magic practitioners as a safety net while casting complex or dangerous spells.

Fae blood ran with magic. They needed visual aids as much as I needed an instruction manual on breathing. I waited, expecting Raven to offer an explanation, but he stared straight ahead with cold determination.

I followed his gaze. Two grotesque fae had materialized on the balcony and now sat in the chairs. Their bodies were humanoid, but their heads were...wrong. One eye the size of a basketball rose from the fleshy stumps of their necks. One had a red iris, the other's was blue.

"No harm will come to you here, child."

The baritone voice beat at me from all sides.

I turned a slow circle. "Who are you, and what right do you have to make such promises?"

Around us thunderous laughter boomed. A burly man limned in green light strode toward us, appearing out of thin air. Bare-chested, he wore leather pants and matching mud-brown boots. A wild nest of hair was drawn into a frizzy knot at his nape. His beard hung in tangles down to his navel with leaves and twigs and burs as accents. He stood two heads taller than me and was three times as wide, his muscles thick and smeared with dried mud.

"I am the Master of the Wild Hunt." A breeze whirled around him smelling of fresh soil and wet dog. "As your father cannot be here, I have come in his stead. I will grant you my protection while you are on these grounds. That is a sight more certain and true than any offer this one can make you."

"He's right." Raven set his jaw. "His word is good. Have no fear of that."

The apparition that was the Huntsman waited until I stepped beside Raven.

Magic sizzled and popped, sealing us inside a protective bubble anchored to the floor by the circle.

"Thierry Thackeray," a voice drifted from the balcony. "We have been expecting you."

I glanced first at the seated fae before my gaze slid past their shoulders to the wall behind them.

Reflections now filled each of the mirrors. Both were sidhe males, both dressed in somber robes. They were visible to us from the waist up, the rest of their bodies obscured by the odd fae sitting before them. The crests above their frames luminesced, revealing ornate designs. One matched Raven's, a raptor with a serpent in its claws, except it faced right-side up. The other showed a stag with enormous antlers wearing a serene expression.

The image in the frame beneath the stag smiled benevolently at me. "I am Consul Liosliath of House Seelie."

Under the raptor crest, Liosliath's counterpart scowled. "I am Consul Daibhidh of House Unseelie."

"You have been informed of our dilemma," Liosliath intoned. "We are most grateful for your consideration in coming here to attempt a mutually beneficial compromise."

Compromise. *Blackmail.* Poh-tay-toh. *Pah-tah-toh.*

"What you do not know," Daibhidh said with a hint of a grin, "is that King Moran is dead."

I jerked my head toward Raven. The king was dead? *Crap.*
Now all the threats and secrecy made sense. A crown was at
stake. Wars had been fought for much less. *Double crap.* The
conclave didn't know. If they had, they would have locked the
threshold down so tight not even a pixie fart could drift through
the wards.

"He was *murdered*," Liosliath corrected. "Therefore, a new
king must be chosen by Right of Hunt."

My breath caught in the vise clamping around my chest.
They meant the Coronation Hunt, the hunt my father had
instituted as a means of determining which house was fit to
rule without rampant bloodshed.

I rubbed my forehead, taking all of it in. "There hasn't been
an assassination since…"

"Not since the Black Dog assembled the High Court and
instituted the Right of Hunt," Daibhidh supplied. "It was his
blood that sealed the contract and brought peace to Faerie. The
Coronation Hunt was his idea, and is his responsibility to
maintain. The Huntsman is prepared, his hounds eager, and yet
Macsen is not here."

"The Sullivan tracks our king's murderer," Liosliath
scolded.

Daibhidh sneered. "He does one duty to the detriment of
another."

The Huntsman exhaled on a snort.

"They can argue for days," he told me in a quiet voice. "The
Seelie want your father to find the king's killer. The Unseelie
want him to lead the hunt so that a new ruler is crowned before
the old one is cold in his grave."

"My mother was taken," I told him just as softly. "She's the
only reason I'm here."

He scratched his beard thoughtfully. "I've heard nothing of
a human in the Halls."

Dread soured the broth in my gut. Mom had to be here. *She
had to be.*

Tired of listening to the consuls bicker, I wanted straight
answers. I just needed to get their attention first.

I tested the bubble with my toe. It held. *I can fix that.*
Murmuring my Word, I removed my glove, and soft light

pooled at my feet. Pushing energy through my hand, I shoved my palm straight up against the dome. Magic hit the reinforced shield, and it exploded outward with a deafening *pop* of air.

Silence fell around me. Into it, I challenged, "I came here to negotiate for the return of my mother."

"Your mother is missing?" Lioslaith's brow furrowed as his reflection glanced at Daibhidh. "Is this House Unseelie's doing?"

Unruffled by the accusation, Daibhidh waved his hand. "For all we know her parents are missing *together*."

"You don't have her?" Doubt dripped from my every word. "Then we have nothing further to discuss."

"Are you saying," Daibhidh crooned, "that you would exchange your life for your mother's?"

"Are you admitting you took her?" I growled under my breath.

"No." His lips twitched. "I have, however, heard things."

I gritted my teeth and played along. "What kind of things?"

"Whispers." His image rippled. "It will cost you to hear them."

Raven gripped my arm. I shrugged him off me. It was his fault I was here in the first place.

"Name your price," I said with more boldness than I felt.

"Gather your father's mantle. Act in his stead. Run in the hunt." Daibhidh's reflection stilled. "Accept his title, become the Black Dog of the Faerie High Court in his absence. Then you can know all that I do. Do you accept?"

Run in the hunt. The blood rushed from my face and left me chilled to the bone. The hunt was a death sentence.

"There must be something else I can offer." Panic raised my voice an octave.

"Are you haggling over your mother's worth?" Daibhidh clicked his tongue.

"No," I snapped, mind whirling. Haggling was exactly what I was about to try.

There must be another way. What else did I have? What else could I do? *What else?*

"Faerie is a dangerous place for a woman to find herself alone. Especially one with such close ties to Macsen Sullivan."

Daibhidh pursed his lips. "Not all fae admire his legacy as we do, you understand, and as Sullivan himself is untouchable... A mortal, well, they are so defenseless, aren't they?"

"She isn't defenseless." Magic leapt into my palm and burned bright. "She has me."

"Ah." He tapped a finger against his bottom lip. "That might be true, but what good are you to her here when she is, well, you don't know where she is, do you?"

I clenched my fist and extinguished my power before I used it and got myself killed ahead of schedule.

"The choice is yours," Daibhidh said. "She might survive Faerie alone. No mortal ever has, but there must always be a first."

Choice? No. This was blackmail, a promise that if I didn't play nice then neither would they, and there was good reason why such tactics were popular among the criminally inclined.

They worked.

"Time grows short. Arrangements must be made soon, whether you are a consideration or not." Liosliath raised his eyebrows. "Have you made your decision?"

A knowing smirk wreathed Daibhidh's face.

My heart beat hard once.

Kill or be killed.

"Yes." I tasted fear when I swallowed. "I'll do it."

Beside me, the Huntsman issued a low growl that rumbled with anticipation.

Tuning him out, I demanded of Daibhidh, "Tell me all you know."

"Your mother is kept safe by an Unseelie loyal to the crown." Daibhidh linked his fingers over his middle. "Once your duty has been done, she will be returned exactly where and how she was found by those who took her." His ageless gaze captured mine. "Before these witnesses, I swear this to you."

I breathed a sigh that left me limp with relief.

Mom was safe. She was going to be okay.

"Thierry." Raven filled my name with anguish.

"Faerie owes you a debt of gratitude." Liosliath visibly relaxed. "As a tradition your father himself established, your participation in the Coronation Hunt ensures it is a legacy in the making."

Tradition.

Legacy.

The magnitude of what I had agreed to crashed over me and left me trembling.

The king was dead. The Huntsman stood at my elbow. And I had just volunteered to play tribute.

Crap, crap, crap.

"This is what the consuls wanted all along," I said under my breath. "This is why you brought me here."

Raven refused to look at me.

But I knew. This was why they sent him to fetch me.

Coronations were held once every one hundred years. According to lore, the purpose of the Wild Hunt was to ride through the mortal realm on All Hallows' Eve, collecting the souls of fae who died on Earth and returning them to Faerie, to the Ever-After, the fae equivalent of Heaven.

On one such hunt, the Huntsman and his pack of sleek, black hounds crossed a battlefield. Their guts were distended with spirit flesh and their hunger temporarily sated when their noses led them to one last feast. Two souls, one Seelie and one Unseelie, stood with their hands clasped as if unaware the hunt was upon them.

The pack leader ran ahead of the others. Confused when the spirits stood their ground, he approached them, sniffed them and allowed each to stroke his silky, midnight fur.

The Seelie held the hound's gaze while the Unseelie spoke. "Only in death have we known peace. If we had raised our voices instead of our swords, much of our grief might have been circumvented. Loyal beast, reaper, it is our final wish that Faerie never endure the misery of another Thousand Years War."

"Mark this day, Black Dog," the Seelie intoned. "Tonight you are the hunter, but one hundred years hence, you shall become the hunted. One prince from each of our houses will hunt you across Faerie wearing the skins of hounds, goaded by your own Huntsman while you wear the skin of a sidhe noble.

Your blood will anoint the new ruler and usher in one hundred more years of prosperity for the fae."

Instead of consuming the spirits as the Huntsman had decreed, Black Dog bowed his head to their will. That simple act of defiance shattered the bonds between himself and the Huntsman, and Black Dog gained awareness. As a gift to aid him in the trials ahead, the Unseelie entered his left eye and the Seelie his right, so that Black Dog might always view both sides of any argument with impartiality.

Black Dog also gained the form of a man so that he might stand toe-to-toe with kings. He named himself Macsen Sullivan and established the Faerie High Court, choosing one Seelie and one Unseelie consul to join him, and instituted the Right of the Hunt.

Once a century, he was run to ground and torn to pieces. The blood of one man was spilled to determine a king. His sacrifice avoided the slaughter of thousands had the houses gone to war for the crown. For the seven days after he was laid to rest in Faerie's soul, the realm mourned him. Lore said those tears seeped into the soil and restored him, and he rose at midnight on the seventh day made whole again.

My father was a legend, and by doing this, I too would go down in history. I just wouldn't get back up again. I was half mortal. The best I could hope for was being long-lived. The immortality thing Mac had going didn't extend to me.

This gave *temp job* a whole new meaning.

Raven stepped forward. "I claim the right of *coimirceoir*."

Both consuls gaped at him.

The Huntsman growled, "On what grounds can you claim guardianship of this girl?"

"She is not a girl, but a woman." Raven set his shoulders back. "She is also my wife."

CHAPTER TWENTY-ONE

Wife? Clearly I wasn't the only one who had sniffed the toadstools.

"She looks surprised to hear you call her that," the Huntsman observed.

The consuls exchanged wary glances.

Liosliath narrowed his eyes. "What proof do you offer of the validity of this union?"

"Thierry has warmed her hands at my hearth, eaten at my table." A pinkish flush crept up Raven's throat. "She has disrobed in my chambers and even now she wears the colors and cuts of my house."

His freaking wife. That was the point of the meal and the clothes and the kindness. Why? What use was I to him or anyone else beyond this point? I had accepted their offer. I was dog chow. Why tighten the noose around my neck?

"We aren't married." Barely suppressed rage trembled through the words.

"She is a Christian. She adopted her mother's faith," Raven explained away my outburst while cutting a shiver-inducing glare my way. "She desires a formal ceremony conducted by her priest before publically acknowledging our union."

"Given her limited knowledge of this realm," the Huntsman murmured, "Rook's familiarity with Faerie would make for a more interesting hunt. I vote yea."

Beware the Rook. The warning clanged in my mind.

"Rook?" I whirled toward Raven. "No. You're Raven, the Morrigan's son."

Daibhidh almost laughed himself off the wall. "Raven is in his rooms upstairs, as any sensible noble would be during these unsettled times. I can introduce you if you like, but you'll meet soon enough."

"He didn't mean the chess piece," I whispered to myself. "A rook...is a bird."

"Rooks are corvids, dear girl, as are all those of the Morrigan's line." Daibhidh wiped a tear from his cheek. "Rook, you are a credit to your family. I was right to trust you with luring Macsen's pup here, but marrying her? You have outdone yourself."

"I am not his wife." The tips of my ears burned. "I didn't consent to any union."

And yet, as I mentally retraced my footsteps through Faerie, I saw each moment leading up to when I stepped neatly into his snare.

I was an idiot.

And Raven—no, *Rook*—was soon to be a widower.

"Be that as it may," Liosliath stated. "I grant Rook's request for guardianship."

"Now that we have that settled." Daibhidh clapped his hands. "Let the hunt begin."

Liosliath inclined his head toward me. "May the best hound win."

A whiff of wet dog told me the Huntsman had shifted closer. "It will be quick, child. I vow that. Go now. Run." He toyed with a leather thong around his neck. Attached was a horn carved from a curving antler. His eyes shone bright in the darkness. He wet his lips then forced his hand to his side. "The hounds are coming."

Shock rooted my feet to the floor. "The hunt starts *now*?"

So much for the Huntsman's vow of protection.

Rook took my hand and yanked me stumbling out of the circle. "Run."

"Are you insane?" I struggled against him. "You're going to get me killed."

"As far as they're concerned, you're already dead." He jerked me so hard my shoulder popped. "This is your only chance."

"Go with him. Hurry, girl." The Huntsman lifted his horn to his lips. "The hunt has begun."

The first blast of his horn made the tile rumble beneath my feet. Toppling off balance, Rook tugged me into motion as the magic in the sound called to me.

Join in the hunt. Blood and bone. Hot and fresh.

My blood. *My* bones.

In answer to the summons, bloodcurdling howls filled the room. The scrabble of nails and the excited barks of a scent picked up turned blood to ice in my veins.

"I have a plan." Rook urged, "Hurry and I might save you yet."

As the barking grew louder in time with the pounding of my heart, God help me, I followed him. For all I knew he was guiding me straight to his brother for an easy kill.

Raven was here, somewhere, waiting. The Wild Hunt's magic would swirl around him and transform him into one of the Huntsman's hounds. Higher reasoning would fade. Only hunger for my blood would drive him.

"You lied to me," I panted. "You're fae. How did you do it?"

"I'm a half-blood." He glanced back. "Like you."

Perfect. I was on the run with the Morrigan's bastard son.

"We can't outrun the hounds." Not real ones. Certainly not the Huntsman's spectral beasts.

How long did I have before the Seelie hound joined Raven—the Unseelie hound—in the hunt?

"I arranged for transport," Rook called. "It's not ideal, but we need a head start."

Afraid to ask for details, I kept my mouth closed. Rook had lied to me from the get-go. Why did I expect honest aid with no strings attached now? Desperation? Anger? Panic? Fear? Yes to all of the above.

The one person who could rescue me was the one shoving my head beneath the waves of the political storm he had helped conjure. I didn't understand his motives. Why not hold me down until the Unseelie hound arrived? If Raven killed me, Unseelie House would rule Faerie and break the Seelie's centuries' long reign.

"This way." Rook changed directions and hauled me after him. "Faster."

"This is as fast as it gets." I was in shape, I had to be for hunting fugitives, but Rook was pro-athlete fit. That or his powers included being as fleet of foot as he was swift of wing.

Through another endless hall we ran, our footsteps covered by the echo of eager hound song. We burst through a boarded door and then staggered out into the snow.

Rook snapped his fingers, and a single black feather appeared between them. "I summon the Morrigan."

"Your mother?" I squeaked. "How are we going to pay her?"

The Morrigan expected payment in flesh for the indignity of answering anyone's summons.

"This feather represents a debt she owes me," he said. "This squares us."

When an earsplitting caw rent the sky over our heads, I covered my ears. "I hope she agrees."

A gargantuan crow landed several yards away. It was larger than the dragons from earlier, and her outstretched wings blotted out the sun.

"That's new." I flinched when she clacked her beak together.

"Mother has many forms." The feather turned to ash in his fingers. "Some, like this, are bound to Faerie."

Good thing too. It was easy to picture her swooping over cities and devouring the citizens if given the chance. She was not a benevolent goddess by any stretch of the imagination. The Morrigan personified war and strife and misery. She reveled in pain, basked in agony and thrilled in the anguish of others.

Taking that into consideration, the notion of the Morrigan as our rescuer was giving me an ulcer.

"Can we trust her?" *Not to eat us.*

"She will do as I ask." He dusted his hands clean. "After that, we have no guarantee she won't fly straight to the Huntsman and tell him where she dropped us."

We approached, and the great crow's beak opened.

The Morrigan's raspy voice issued from its throat. "Rook."

"Mother." He inclined his head. "The favor I ask of you is your aid in escorting us safely to the edge of Autumn."

"You ask much of me, my son." Her beady eyes raked over me. "Thierry Thackeray. You have been good to me. Therefore, I will grant this one-time aid. I will fly you and my child to the edge of Autumn, where I must leave you to your fate." She rustled her feathers and puffed up at Rook. "Are these terms agreeable to you?"

"They are." Rook kissed his pointer finger and faced it toward her in salute.

I fumbled for the right words to frame my gratitude. "Your help is much appreciated."

"Oh, it is more than worth it to me." A cackle rose from her throat. "I owed Rook a debt much larger than the paltry favor he is content to redeem it for. Had he asked first, I might have done this for free."

"You do nothing for free," he said lightly. "Let us not pretend otherwise."

He boosted me onto her back and then climbed up behind me.

The Morrigan vibrated beneath us with her laughter. "Now, son, you'll give Thierry the wrong impression of her mother-in-law."

I glared at Rook over my shoulder and mouthed, *We aren't married.*

A tight smile stretched his lips as he linked his hands at my navel. The caress of his thumbs sent quivers through my stomach. I was queasy. That was it. Or grateful, which was worse. He was not tempting me. Well, okay, tempting me to wring his neck, yes. Tempting me to jump his bones, no. Just so we're clear.

"Hold on." The Morrigan spread her vast wings and launched into the sky.

Beneath us, frustrated barks stung my ears as a dozen hounds loped after us.

One hound leapt, snapping his jaws close to her tail. Without warning, she cried out and swooped, catching the dog before its front paws hit the ground, tossing her head back as she gulped him down with a satisfied chirrup. Price paid. Belly taut with dog flesh, the Morrigan soared.

Whirling snow gave way to flurrying leaves below us as the frigid air warmed by several degrees. I had a bird's-eye view for the changing of the seasons, and it was breathtaking. Soaring over the seasonal divide was like flipping channels from black-and-white melodrama to full Technicolor extravaganza.

Red and orange treetops popped against the browning grasses. Autumn was, as far as I could tell, one endless forest. What an ideal place for a hunt.

Rook's arms tightened around me before I sensed the subtle variance in our altitude.

"This is as far as I will go," the Morrigan said. "Have a care, son. Die well, daughter."

The great crow dipped lower, until her wake made the leaves tremble.

"Hold on to me," Rook murmured against my neck. "This is where we get off."

Scenery zipped under us. "Um, she isn't slowing down."

His sympathetic look might have earned him more points if his mother hadn't chosen that exact moment to disembark us by executing a barrel roll. I fisted her feathers and held on for dear life. She squawked and shrugged, sending us into a tailspin. The harder I yanked, the faster we dove.

Rook's hands covered mine. "We have to jump."

"Are you insane?" I screamed. "She won't kill herself to get rid of us."

"You don't know my mother. Death is a temporary inconvenience as far as she's concerned."

Meaning she came back the same as Macsen did. Great. Everyone here was immortal but me.

Even with the ground racing up to meet me, I stubbornly clung to her back.

"Let go." Rook yanked on my hands, ripping out fistfuls of feathers. "Thierry, please."

Fingers sweaty, I lost my hold. He clasped my hands before I could grasp another anchor.

"Good girl," he breathed, tightening his grip on me and letting go for both of us.

For an eternity, we dangled from the Morrigan's back by the strength of my thighs as I clenched her sides, but Rook was heavy and so was I. The material of my pants conspired against me, and our weight sucked me from the back of the great bird and sent us hurtling downward toward the spiky treetops.

Leaves swatted me in the face and limbs caught my hair. Rook drew me closer, tried to protect me from the worst of it, but the fall was harsh. Landing was worse. Rook hit flat on his back, winded but whole. Impact jarred my right side, and that arm went numb. I coughed against the damp ground.

"Is anything broken?" He still rested on his back, gazing into the canopy of trees.

"I can't feel my right arm." I rolled onto my back, grinding my teeth while I flexed my fingers. When that didn't kill me, I raised my arm. "Not broken." I twisted my head toward him. "How about you?"

"I'm fine." He sat up with his left arm tucked against his chest. "We have to move."

I pushed onto my knees, drew back my left arm and punched him square in the nose. "That was for lying to me."

Blood trickled over his lips, down his chin. "Are you finished?"

"For now." I shoved onto my feet. "I reserve the right to change my mind later."

Rook rolled onto his feet too, still cradling his arm.

"You aren't fine." I shook out my hand. "Your arm is broken."

"It will mend itself." He drew his cloak around him. "We must keep moving."

He set out, certain I would follow. And I did. What choice did I have?

With a sigh, I trailed after him. "I don't understand the game you're playing."

"I can scarcely keep track of it myself." He didn't slow to welcome conversation. "I regret drawing you into this plot, I regret deceiving you, but your father's disappearance presented the High Court with an opportunity, and they used me to seize it."

I slowed as a thought occurred to me. "Was the Morrigan in on it?"

He chuckled. "Who do you think taught me how to cross the threshold?"

Oh snap. The conclave would have kittens over this.

Still amused, he asked, "Is there anything else you would like to know?"

As a matter of fact... "Tell me about the hunt."

"That's rather grim, don't you think?"

"Is the lore true?" I pressed. "One prince from each house will take the form of a hound?"

"Yes."

"Back there—that was more than two hounds."

"The princes are made honorary pack members during the hunt. The Huntsman runs them all for the thrill of it, and to ensure their prey doesn't escape. Macsen knows Faerie better than anyone. If it was an honest fight between him and the princes, well, Faerie would have been under his rule since his awakening."

Huh. I never considered he could win but chose not to.

Though I guess a sacrifice wasn't a sacrifice unless you paid for it dearly.

"Once the pack corners their quarry," he continued, "the princes fight it out among themselves for the right to make the crown-winning kill. Assuming both princes have survived to that point. Both princes don't always live to the end."

"Okay, so the princes are the real threat." That was unexpected good news. "Raven is the Unseelie hound. Who is the other?"

"Riordan." Pity laced his tone. "King Moran was his father."

"Great." Heirs were never more dangerous than when grieving or desperate to restore their family to glory. "Have I mentioned how much I appreciate you dragging me into this mess, Rook?" I snorted. "If that is your real name."

"You heard my mother call me by that name," he said flatly. "She is full-blooded and can't lie."

"Maybe not, but someone told me once fae tell the truth so well it might as well be a lie."

"I deserve your distrust, but can't you accept I want to help you? Haven't I given you proof?"

"The more proof you show me, the closer I have to inspect the fine print." Rook had proven to me where his loyalties lay. "Have you helped me? Yes. Do I believe you burned a favor from the Morrigan to rescue me out of the goodness of your heart? No. Your brother is a hound. He's hunting me even now. If he kills me, your house will rule. You must want that. Why else would you drag me into this?"

He whirled on me. "I am your *coimirceoir*."

"My guardian, I got that." I shoved him. "That was very slick how you managed to make sure you got stuck with me out here. It will come in handy for leaving breadcrumbs for your brother to follow."

"You don't understand. That's not how this works."

"Explain it then, because I'm a little confused about what the hell it is you think you're doing."

"As your husband, you are safe from me." He exhaled. "I can't be used against you again."

"Then why claim guardianship? If naming me as your wife absolved you, why take out extra insurance?"

His lips mashed into a stubborn line and held for so long I was almost startled when he spoke.

"If your mother is returned to you unharmed, and you yourself return unharmed, then I have done no wrong for which I should be ashamed." Rook bent closer and whispered in my ear, "My plan, *wife*, is to find your father before the hounds find you. He can trade places with you. He can run the hunt, die as the new prince is crowned and then rise to snarl over your involvement later."

Dangerous hope sparked in my chest. "Do you know where he is?"

"No." He jerked his chin in the direction we had been going. "He was last seen near here."

Gooseflesh rippled over my skin. "Why are you doing this?"

"I have my reasons."

"Reasons you won't share."

"Either you accept I mean no harm or assume I am as treacherous as I have given you every reason to believe." He rolled his shoulders. "Either way, I'm not waiting for the hounds to reach us. The princes might want you in particular, but the others will be less choosy. You must decide if you can trust me that far or if you should go your own way."

Rook left me standing in dappled sunlight. The turning leaves were no longer beautiful to me. The oranges were too bright and the reds called to mind the blood that would soon spill.

I wrapped my arms around myself and wished Mai was here. A sly fox would know how to outsmart those hounds. Wishing wouldn't make her appear, so I filled my lungs with crisp fall air and exhaled out my fears and doubts.

Think. Frame this problem like it was an exercise dreamed up by Shaw.

Rook might help me find Mac. He might not. Safer to bet not. It seemed to me that if Rook or anyone else knew where Mac was, I wouldn't be here. Nails biting into my elbows where I cupped them, I forced my shoulders to relax. Lowering my arms, I swung them to limber up and tugged on my glove from habit.

My glove.

My runes.

I could rend and devour souls. If I defeated the princes, I might survive the hunt. At least until the next set of heirs were named. Then the consuls would have to renegotiate terms with me, right? I hadn't agreed to substitute eternally, just this once.

Weak as it was, that sounded almost like a plan.

I might not be kibble yet after all.

CHAPTER TWENTY-TWO

Rook must have anticipated my change of heart. That or he enjoyed shuffling his feet in leaves. It took all of five minutes to catch up, and when I did, the only acknowledgment he gave was picking up his pace. Content as I could be with my cut-and-paste survival plan, I fell in line behind him.

Hours later, without much progress, shadows began waking, stretching toward us from the bases of the trees. The air turned cooler. Not winter cold, but chill enough I was grateful for the heat spell on my armor.

Music stirred in the air, sweet singing that twitched in my toes as I walked.

When I couldn't stand the silence another minute, I jogged to Rook's side. "Do you hear that?"

"Ignore it as best you can. It's a lure the dryads use." His eyes roved over me. "They're Seelie."

I shivered. "They're trying to ensnare me."

"It's in their best interest if the Seelie continue to rule." He cautioned, "Stay clear of the trees."

His gaze slid past my shoulder, prompting me to search for what had captured his attention. Superimposed over the trunk of the nearest tree was a pale blue outline of a nude woman. Her arms were raised above her head, lifting her pert breasts and accentuating the fluid curve of her waist and soft roundness of her hips. She stood with one thigh in front of the other, hinting at hidden pleasures.

I was enchanted, had taken a step closer before the sap-sweet scent of her lure enveloped me. A sneezing fit seized me, blasting the scent out of my nose and clearing my head.

Guess I owed Shaw a case of ginger beer. Exposure to his lure must have inoculated me against other variants. Fighting hers was easy. Resisting Shaw? Now that was hard.

Rook stood his ground, eyes glazed while the dryad worked her enchantment.

If I wanted to be rid of him, this was a prime opportunity. I could leave him here with little miss bark for boobs and see how far I got before the hounds sniffed me out and I put my theory to the test.

I made it three steps before guilt gnawed through my resolve. I turned back and found Rook nearer the dryad. Much closer and he would reach out. If he touched her, she would use him for fertilizer.

"Rook."

He didn't blink.

"*Rook.*"

Blank stare ahoy.

The dryad's lips never moved, but the soft music continued drifting around us. Strange behavior for a tree spirit. From what I remembered in my old textbooks, they were peace-loving, live-and-let-live types. Sirens were more into lethal musical snares. The two could be related I guess, but the dryad's urgent song still struck me as odd.

The Coronation Hunt must bring out the teeth in everyone.

Easing between them, I broke Rook's eye contact with her. Sound was the problem. Earplugs. That was what I needed. Checking his pockets, I found them as empty as mine. Casting around for something I could use, I spotted clumps of thick moss covering the roots of a nearby tree. "Don't move, okay?"

He gave no indication he heard me. He hadn't moved since I stepped between them.

As fast as I could, I darted to the tree and scooped a handful of moss from the ground. I gave the spongy green stuff a test squeeze. The texture was foamy, but it was slower to reclaim its former shape. Guess I would have to pack it in his ear canals tighter then.

Rolling the topmost moss into tiny pellets, I did the best I could with what I had. Rook still hadn't moved. He didn't make a peep when I crammed the makeshift plugs in his ears, either. Feeling time slip through my fingers, I battled a sense of urgency to ditch him and keep moving. My endgame might be facing down those hounds, but I wasn't going to make it easy for them.

After a few moments, Rook blinked.

"Hello." I waved my hand in front of his face. "Anyone home?"

He focused on me, or he tried to. His gaze ping ponged between me and the dryad.

"Let's get moving, okay?" I yelled.

His slow nod told me he was coming around. Good. We had wasted too much time as it was.

Adrenaline drenched me in a sudden rush that left my nerves taut and my thighs trembling with the urge to run. I scented the cool, clean air. Decomposing leaves. Rich earth. Nothing out of the ordinary, even by Faerie standards. The hairs on the back of my neck lifted, but I was done waiting.

"If whatever it is wants to kill us," I told Rook quietly, "it'll just have to take a number and get in line."

Linking my arm through his, I led a dreamy-eyed Rook ambling down a path through the trees. I hadn't noticed it before, and it was more of an animal run than a man-made road, but the dirt beneath the day's accumulation of leaves was hard packed and well worn. Someone must be using it often.

"Thierry." He slurred my name. "I need to—"

He exploded in a blast of feathers.

"Rook?" I spun in a circle, clutching quills in my hands like that would help.

A caw overhead made my shoulders slump. He flapped harder until he pierced the canopy. Great. Some guardian he was.

Alone in the forest, I dusted my hands and trudged onward. Night drifted around me, cooler and darker, hungrier. Common sense said I ought to seek shelter. Stopping for the night wasn't appealing when I had already lost so much time. If Rook came back, I could ask how long these hunts lasted.

Something told me not long. I figured I had twenty-four hours at most.

"You look awful tired, yes?" a tinny voice called. "I have a bed. Food. I have that too."

I slowed my steps. "Show yourself."

"Sure. I can do." A small black rabbit hopped out of the woods. "See? No harm, dog girl."

I crossed my arms. "Dog girl?"

"Word spreads fast." He thumped his back foot. "Old king is dead. The hunt runs tonight."

Considering the dryad attack, yeah, gossip must be burning up the vines out here.

Anxious to get moving, I cut to the chase. "Why would you help me?"

"Rook Morriganson sent me." His whiskers twitched. "He said to take you to the burrow."

"I wish I believed you, little guy." I sighed and walked past him. "I just can't risk it."

A blast of scalding magic slammed into my back.

"You will come." The rabbit's voice dropped several octaves. "I gave my word. In exchange, he swore you would return my brother to me. He lives where you live now. Goes by the name Sean."

"I can't prison-break your brother then look the other way while he dials the windmill."

"Rook said. He told me you would help," he trumpeted. "You *will* help."

I spun, ready to punt the fur face and move on, except the fluffy bunny was gone, replaced by the tallest horse I had ever seen. Twenty hands high if he was an inch. Broad too, built like a draft horse.

"You're a púca." Karma really was a bitch.

The horse executed a bow that brought its eyes level with mine. "Want a ride?"

"Do I have a choice?" That thing could trample me.

He nickered. "I am helping. Then you will help. We can be friends now. Climb aboard."

"I've never ridden a—" He kept bending until he knelt on the ground. "Well. Okay then." After circling around to his side, I fisted his mane and climbed on his back.

When the horse rose, I gulped down a knot of panic. This was almost worse than riding the Morrigan's back. Gliding through the air had been fun right up until the near-death landing experience. Down here it was duck or let the low-slung branches knock the head off my shoulders.

Without a saddle, I kept sliding to one side. The best I could do was clutch the tufts of his mane and clench my thighs. The púca executed a slight hop step over a fallen limb that almost unseated me. My stomach flip-flopped until I flattened against his spine and pressed my face to his neck.

Maybe Rook was right. Maybe Macsen had done me a favor by allowing Mom to raise me as a human. Faerie was so alien. I hated how it made me feel weak, like prey.

Fae in my world, I could handle. I knew the rules there. Here all bets were off. When I got home, *if* I got home, I was kissing the first plain old, non-magical dirt clod I found.

Sensing how tender my stomach was, the púca showed mercy and ambled the final yards to our destination. "Down you go," he said with a snort. He knelt, and I slid onto jelly legs.

"Where are we?" I hadn't noticed on the way in, but this section of forest seemed greener.

"Near the border of Spring." A wave of magic rolled over him. "We're safe enough here."

While brushing off the residue of his change, I noticed he had reverted to his rabbit form.

"Hurry it up. Hop to it." His long ears rotated while his nose wrinkled. "Someone's coming."

I sensed the same eerie presence as before. "Where am I hurrying to?"

"The burrows of course." He jumped up and down. "Well. Shift. Come on. Move it along."

"Shift? As in shapeshift?" I cocked an eyebrow at him. "I can't."

"You don't have a smaller skin than that?" He sounded incredulous.

"What are you talking about?" His brain must have shrunk too. "This is the only skin I have."

"This won't do." He rubbed one paw with the other. "You're too big. Enormous."

"Thanks." I exhaled through my teeth. "Now what?"

"He's here." His eyes rounded at the base of a distant tree. "You're on your own."

With a flash of his tail, the púca vanished into a shadowy hole, leaving me alone. Again.

While I debated whether to return to Autumn, the sensation of being watched turned overwhelming. "Who's out there?" I called where the púca had been staring.

"A bystander," an ominous voice rumbled, "nothing more."

"Great." My teeth began chattering. "Who knew death was the ultimate spectator sport?"

If the creature who had spoken remained, he deigned not answer me.

Over my head in the pitch-black sky, a sharp cry sounded. A trim black bird landed between me and the voice in the woods, hop-stepping until he stood by my side.

"I tried." The púca's voice startled me. Pink eyes peered from the mouth of a tunnel. "She can't shift." He ventured out to greet us. "No one said she couldn't."

The black bird bobbed its head, and the púca's narrow shoulders slumped.

"When I get home—" *if I got home*, "—I'll talk to your brother, okay? No promises."

The fur face somersaulted into the air. "With my thanks."

Huh. Go figure. I had just earned a favor I could call in later. First time for everything.

Once the púca darted into its burrow, Rook rustled his feathers.

"Don't look at me like that." I scowled at the fidgety bird, who cocked his head at me. "We both know chances are slim I'll come out the other side of this. Why not give the little guy some hope?"

The bird spread his wings and hopped toward the base of the nearest tree. I took the hint and followed. I started regretting my decision when he fluttered onto the lowest limb and waited. For me to join him.

"I hope you know what you're doing."

He hopped the length of his perch in answer.

Living in a pinprick southern town out in the middle of nowhere, I had plenty of experience climbing trees. I stood under the limb and jumped. When I had a firm grip, I pulled myself up beside him. I shouldn't have grinned. The second I did, he hopped onto the next limb and sat there, waiting.

It was going to be a long night.

It was still dark when I woke. Only a few hours had passed because my head throbbed from lack of sleep. I functioned better running on fumes than when I stole too little shut-eye. I always woke up more tired than I was to start with, and grumpier to boot. A low growl rose in my throat while I tried pinpointing what had roused me. Not the hounds. Not another dryad or a púca or the sensation of being watched.

No. The unexpected comfort had done it. That soft puff of breath at my ear helped too.

The cradle of limbs where I had fallen asleep held high above the forest, lashed to the tree trunk with my cape just in case, had been itchy, scratchy and hard. My current situation lacked two out of three of those amenities.

Blood rushed into my cheeks when I realized why I was so warm and what was jabbing my hip.

Rook reclined between the limbs, comfortable as any other bird in a tree.

During the night, he had pulled me onto his lap, wrapped his calves over my legs and cinched his arms around my waist. Attempting to evaluate the situation, I twisted to my left, where I was rewarded with a glimpse of him sleeping. His eyes were closed, and he was easier to see that way. At rest, he looked more like a man, though still an achingly handsome one. Not at all like he was a liar or a manipulator.

"You were fidgeting," he murmured. "I was afraid you would fall."

I tensed, and his grip tightened. "Where did you go?"

"Not far." He kept his eyes closed like he knew what I had been thinking. "The dryad was luring my human half. The swiftest cure was to shift forms. I should have done it immediately, but I was—"

"Eyeing her boobs?" I supplied.

His chuckles rumbled through my side. "She did have a lovely set of...pinecones."

I elbowed his gut. "Only a man would forgive attempted murder in exchange for a peep show."

His fingers stroked up my arm. "You saved me."

"I know." I fought shivers from his touch. "I don't know what I was thinking."

"That you need me." He traced the line of dancing chills. "Or maybe you even like me."

"Ha." I planted my elbow square in his chest for leverage. "Liking you is the last thing I can afford to do, even if you weren't a kidnapper, a liar—oh yeah—and the orchestrator of my impending doom. That last one was awesome, by the way."

His gentle caresses stopped. "Why did you join the marshals?"

I drew back to look at him. "What does that matter?"

"Humor me."

"The short answer is, if I hadn't signed up, the conclave would have killed me." Saying it out loud left a bad taste in my mouth.

He cocked his head at me. "What's the long answer?"

I debated whether to tell him, but the peaceful night lent itself to sharing secrets. "When I showed up on their doorstep asking for sanctuary, I was just a kid. Thirteen with blood on my hands. They offered me a life I couldn't have had on my own. They put me in a private school for fae children and helped me adjust to my new normal.

"When I graduated high school, I was given a choice. Enroll in the marshal academy, where they could put my talents to good use, or get put down. Apparently, they couldn't afford to have someone like me running around unchecked." I shrugged like it still didn't hurt when I thought about it. "At first, it was about saving my bacon. Now it's...atonement...I guess."

"How did you know to contact them? Macsen never let on he had a daughter."

He knew the answer, I could tell by the lack of inflection in his tone.

"He told Mom who to call if things got bad," I said quietly. "When I got into the kind of trouble that meant I would have been locked up for the rest of my life, she dialed the number, and the conclave sent Shaw to fetch me. They saved me. They gave me a higher purpose."

"Do you enjoy your work?"

"I do." The honesty of my answer surprised me. "Humans fall prey to creatures they don't stand a chance against. I like making fae think twice before breaking the law in my region." What I didn't confess was how much the hunter in me enjoyed the pursuit. Or how well suited my gifts were to my trade. Rook was perceptive. He would guess even if I didn't confirm it for him. "I like helping people."

"Humans aren't the only ones in need of help." His lips parted, but he said nothing more.

"Tell me something I don't know." Humans could be just as screwed up as fae. I knew that better than most. "But anything inhuman has the strength and resources to have a fighting chance. Most humans don't."

His forehead creased. "Does that include you?"

I mashed my lips together. "That's what I get for making sweeping generalizations."

"I'm curious." He adjusted under my weight, calling attention to the fact I still sat on his lap.

"I haven't got it all figured out, but I do okay." I admitted, "Or I did until I met you."

I untangled our limbs and pushed off his chest.

His hand circled my wrist. "A few minutes more."

After a moment's hesitation, where I decided he was more comfortable than a tree limb, I let him drag me back down. "What do you know about bystanders in regard to the hunt? I met one last night."

"Ah. You saw them earlier, at the Halls."

"The googly-eyed things guarding the mirrors, right?"

"Yes." He chuckled. "They're called Watchers and travel in pairs. They're the eyes of their respective houses. Each records the hunt for review later in case there are any disputes about the outcome."

Great. All my bumbling recorded for posterity. "What was the deal with those mirrors anyway?"

"The consuls are great powers." Rook toyed with the frazzled ends of my hair. "They are strong enough to project their likeness or voice anywhere they wish. They never attend hearings in the flesh. With the exception of your father, I don't know of a single fae who has ever met them."

Interesting. "The Watchers are the consuls' guardians?"

He waited a moment before answering, "Yes."

"The one I encountered felt powerful." More powerful than it had at the meeting.

"They draw on the power of the house they serve," he explained. "They aren't a threat to you."

"That makes two who aren't," I grumbled.

For once Rook didn't protest that he wasn't a threat, and for once I wondered if perhaps he wasn't.

Was he bound in service to his brother's house the way I was bound to the conclave? Live or die. Easy choice. Even if choosing life meant doing things that once appalled you. At least you were alive. You had, if not the opportunity for change, the hope for it. You had reasons to keep you going.

How could I blame Rook if he was under the same sanctions as I was?

My duty to the mortal realm was to maintain peace at any cost. That I was a death dealer meant that kind of maintenance came naturally to me. Rook was death-touched too. Now that I knew he was a half-blood like me, I had no doubt there had been a steep price for him surviving this extraordinary world.

Ancient as he claimed to be—and his weary eyes dated him—he was a hardcore survivor. I didn't see him ceding his battle in the foreseeable future, not to me or on my behalf.

Old things got old by being smart and not making waves.

My coming here caused a splash and sent ripples through Faerie's stagnant waters. Rook's hand might not push me under, but holding on to his arm wouldn't keep my head above water either. It hit me whoever sent him might have thought his muddied bloodlines would help win me over, that I might trust a half-blood more readily than a pure-blooded fae. I guess *Raven* had thought otherwise.

No time like the present to ask. "Why did you tell me you were Raven?"

"I never said I was. I said I was the Morrigan's son, and you assumed I meant Raven." He voice grew a sharp edge. "I thought if I went to you as a prince, you would be more inclined to help. I see now I was wrong, but what's done is done."

"Everyone knows my father too." I patted his chest. "That doesn't make it cool to namedrop."

I pushed off his shoulders and situated myself on the rough limb beside him.

A fierce grumble made Rook bolt upright.

"False alarm." I put a hand to my stomach. "We should have packed supplies before we left."

"The hunt…" His voice trailed into silence.

"Doesn't last long enough to bother with food or other niceties," I finished for him.

Pleasant as our stolen moment had been, talk of the hunt made me twitchy. I had to move. I needed to pace, to walk, to do something other than make myself a sitting target.

Climbing the tree went faster in reverse. I hit the ground and stretched out the kinks in my back and shoulders while Rook cheated his way down by sprouting wings and gliding onto my shoulder. Considering how smooth his flight was, his broken arm must have healed without any complications. He was heavier as a bird than I expected. Curiosity won out, and I reached up to stroke his chest.

I grinned as his beak worried the pad of my finger. "Are you scouting ahead or sprouting legs?"

Rook cawed and shoved off my hand, flapping his wings until he vanished from sight.

The cramps in my legs thanked me when I started walking.

While Rook was about his business, I decided I should get serious with mine. Trees were nice, but yesterday's dryad encounter convinced me they were not the safest place to make my stand. One spirit in the right place could shove me off a branch or—as an extreme measure—another equally invested fae could chop down my refuge.

Autumn's endless forest gave dryads plenty of options for their next sensual attack. Winter was out of the question. No death wish here. That left my options as Summer, which would be out for blood to reclaim the Seelie throne, and Spring. I was betting Spring was where the tether spat us out into Faerie.

That made it as close to home as I might ever be again.

Between the singing toadstools and all the slithering vines, the hounds and I would be at an equal disadvantage there. Surviving in Spring might prove as difficult as fending off the beasts. Not a boost for my slim odds, but at least I wasn't rolling belly up either. It could work. Now I only had to get there.

The púca said his burrow was near the border, so I angled my brisk walk in that direction.

Only when I became breathless did I realize how fast I was going. Tingles swept over me when I stopped to ease the catch in my side. Ahead, the forest thinned and the ground turned green and bursting with life. Already my ears caught the mashup of birdsong, enchanted melodies and the chirp of rowdy crickets.

The urge to run tensed my calves as the first howl echoed through the forest.

I inhaled but smelled nothing. Spirits had scents. The hunt must be masking theirs. Too bad I hadn't been able to do the same. Gulping the panic coating the back of my throat, I ran for Spring. I passed potential weapons, but kept going. Fear chipped away at my plans, urged me not to think but to flee. I hit the edge of Spring and sighed as if crossing that invisible line made any difference.

A blur to my right surprised a scream out of me before I realized it was Rook and not a hound.

Clutched in his talons hung a limp rabbit…a pinkish one.

"You go ahead." I spotted a large boulder. "I'm not hungry."

Rook dove in front of me, causing me to stumble, before he darted toward the rock. He met me on the highest peak, nudging the corpse toward me with his beak. He flexed his wings until I lifted it.

"I don't understand." Holding it gave me the willies. "What do you want me to do?"

A throb of power banished the bird and left a swirl of magic at my elbow.

"Skin it," Rook ordered.

An eager howl made me flinch. "Fine." Anything to get us moving again.

After reciting my Word, I removed my glove. Transferring the rabbit into my left hand, I fed a steady stream of magic into its limp body. This time there was no pain to share as my power scissored beneath its skin, slicing the mottled fur away from the muscles. The pelt slid from the body into my hand.

"I don't understand." I ran my fingers over the silky fur. "The pelt...it's soft." Usually my talent sucked the skins dry and left me holding flaky husks.

Whatever its faults were, Faerie agreed with my magic.

Barking shook me from my confusion, and I flung the corpse to the ground hoping the treat would earn me a few minutes more.

"Your father is dual natured. Man and hound, they wear many faces," Rook hurried. "I thought the talent skipped a generation since you never shift, but that was before I learned you'd had no contact with your father. Perhaps you have the gift too and just don't know how to use it."

"You want me to shift too?" I lifted the pelt. "Into this?"

"Your father is a hound in the guise of a man, but that is not his only skin. Tricks keep the hunts lively, and that was one of his favorites." Rook placed his hands on my shoulders. "I hoped we could find your father before now, that word would spread and he would come for you. We could have asked him how the shape shift was done, but we're out of time. You must try. Or you will die here."

CHAPTER TWENTY-THREE

Clutching the skin in my shaky hands, I met Rook's gaze. His eyes darkened and thunder rolled when he spoke, jarring me from the vise clamping around my chest.

"Eyes are windows to the soul." His voice rang with profound meaning I couldn't grasp.

Deep-chested baying alerted us to the approaching pack.

Sweat trickled between my shoulder blades.

"Curtains are half off at JCPenney," I snapped. "What's your point?"

Rook took the pelt out of my hands, draped the fur over my head and tugged the face down so I looked through the lopsided slits where the rabbit's eyes had been.

My view of the world—distorted.

Down, down, down, the swirling wisps of ancient magic dragged me.

I reached up to adjust the skin, but it was stuck. The sensation of drowning worsened until the only thing I could do was cough, certain my lungs were filling with water and the next second would be my last. I would have slid off the boulder if Rook hadn't clutched my shoulders and held on tight.

"What's—" I gasped, "—happening?"

Concern warred with his features but relief won. "You're shifting."

Pain whispered over every inch of my skin until furious tears were wrung from my eyes. Sore as I was, I welcomed Rook's embrace. I clung to him, burying my face against his chest while my flesh ignited in a searing rush.

"How did…?" My mouth stopped working. My lips were wrong and words wouldn't come. Still he understood.

"I wasn't born this way. I might have lived and died as a mortal if I had been allowed to remain with my father, but the Morrigan came for me the year I stood on the cusp of manhood. She claimed me as her son and told me I must kill a rook, my namesake, and claim its form as my own. If you shift enough times, a skin becomes yours." His tone went soft. "Mother told me while I was young and powerless that if I couldn't fly away, I would be eaten."

Nice mother you've got there. Of course, my father was no prize either.

At least the Morrigan had come for Rook, taken him in hand and taught him to survive. The survival thing…wasn't working out so well for me.

"Shh." Rook stroked down my back. "Don't struggle."

I couldn't help myself. I thrashed, kicking him harder the tighter he restrained me. I braced my hind legs on his chest… *Hind legs?* What—?

I flexed my hands. Make that front paws.

Well, I'll be damned. It worked. It actually worked.

"I'm going to carry you, all right?" Rook pointed at the neighboring boulder. "We need to circle back to Autumn. There's another entrance to the burrow on the other side." I swiveled an ear at him, curious how he knew. "I've hunted púcas before." He shrugged. "It amused Mother when I was a mastering my skin."

He must have meant catching the púca before it shifted into something able to give a young rook a run for his money. Poor things. That explained how Rook knew where to seek shelter last night too, but not why they welcomed him.

Though I suppose fear he might get a sudden hankering for rabbit was a powerful motivator.

"We don't have time for you to learn this form." He stroked my ears, eliciting an excited thump from my rear leg and a brief grin from him. "I'll carry you as far as I can before I shift, then we run."

Safe in the cradle of Rook's arms, I studied the boulder where he stood. It was the lower section of a larger chain than I first thought. As he climbed, more stone revealed itself. The higher he climbed, the taller the peaks loomed. Enchanted rock, it had to be. Rook must have reached the same conclusion.

He paused to catch his breath and turned to see how far we had come, and barked a tired laugh.

We hadn't gone anywhere.

It was all an illusion.

Rook stood on the same boulder, at the same height as where we started.

"I have a new plan." He tucked me snugly under his arm. "I will make a run for it."

Afraid to fight him, worried I might fall and be snapped up by the jaws of a hound, I curled into a tight ball and prayed.

The hunting pack, whose enthusiastic pursuit carried in surround sound—thus making it impossible to pinpoint their location, another nasty trick that was starting to piss me off—burst into view the instant Rook's feet hit the ground. Those bastards. They must have caught up while we were stuck in that blasted rock illusion.

My first glimpse of them made me quiver. I counted a dozen beasts. All wore thick black fur and each emitted a familiar green light. The faint glow was identical to the runes covering my palm.

Two dogs stood taller than the rest. They shouldered through the middle of the pack, paused to snarl a warning at the others and then lunged for Rook. He spun aside, missing the first hound's jaws but not escaping the second. Its growl reverberated through Rook's chest to my ear. That prince was vicious.

I knew to the marrow of my bones that beast was Raven and that this attack was a warning.

The scent of blood, dulled through the filter of the rabbit's skin, told me Rook was injured. Grunting through the pain, Rook knocked the hound aside and sprinted around the stone. His heavy breaths mirrored mine. My feet tapped in a sympathetic rhythm.

Faster. Faster. *Hurry.*

The thump of padded feet on mossy ground pursued us. Eager cries lifted the hairs all over my body. Shivering awareness set my whiskers twitching. The sensation of being watched rushed over me, bristling my fur.

In the darkness ahead, I spied two gleaming eyes. One to either side of the trees.

One eye was a tranquil blue, the other a simmering red. Watchers then. Both of them.

Their arrival heralded an avalanche of doubts. What did they know we didn't? Was this the end? Was a trap set ahead? Were we running toward it? Were they watching a predestined event? Death elevated for their entertainment?

Rook skidded as he rounded a squat tree. A yelp rose behind us as a hound smashed into the trunk.

I wanted to pump my fist. I did grin up at him. Even if he spared a glance down, and he didn't, I felt pretty sure that the bunny equivalent of a smile was more spastic nose aerobics. Muscles in my face weren't used to all the phantom muscle memory embedded in this skin. Not that I wouldn't take nasal discomfort over, well, imminent death.

Bunny brain must be a thing. All I needed was fluff in my head while we were in danger.

We.

Rook had taken a hit for me. He could have flung me at the dogs and ran or shifted and flown into the welcoming skies. But he hadn't. He had stayed. He was running for our lives to reach púca sanctuary.

I pressed my face against his shirt and breathed in his smoky scent.

Nudging my mind toward clarity, I prepared myself. The burrow entrance wasn't far from here. I had to be ready to bolt when my paws hit dirt.

Rook could shift in a blink. The learning curve was all mine.

"Between those two oaks," Rook panted. "Do you see the brambles? When I set you down, run left. The entrance is underneath a sprig of holly. Follow the tunnel until you reach the commons." He clutched me tighter. "Wait for me there. If something happens… I'm sorry I brought you into this."

I dug my claws into his arm, clinging to him. I didn't want to let go. But I had to. The hounds snapped on his heels. The time it would take him to shift, he would lose by getting me near the briar hedge. At least if he socked me away, he could take wing. He was better off alone. Without me, the beasts would release him unscathed. It wasn't his blood they craved.

Rook's stride hitched. Vicious growls rose up behind him. Impact jarred me out of his arms and sent me tumbling across the ground. I landed on all fours facing him. The same hound as before tore into Rook's back, shredding his cloak and gnawing on the light armor. I twisted to run, tried to go. I couldn't. My rabbit's heart beat so hard my chest ached and black spots swam in my vision.

The predator in me snarled. This was not me. I was not this weak or this pathetic. I was not prey.

Rook sank his elbow into the hound's muzzle, sat up and located me. "Go, Thierry. Run. Stay safe."

Stay safe. I owed him that.

Running didn't work. This body lacked that function. Hopping. That was what rabbits did. They evaded danger, not confronted it. Locking down that mentality, I kicked off with my hind legs and launched myself face-first into the dirt. Spitting dirt, I tried again and face-planted again.

Giving up on the dream of leaping to safety, I pushed onto all fours and focused on coordinating a shuffling hop step. It worked. I covered a foot. Two feet. Three. Four. Five. I was going to make it.

Behind me the snapping of teeth set my fur on edge.

Block it out. Keep going. Head down, eyes forward. *Be the bunny.*

The brambles waited ahead. I skirted the perimeter in search of the holly sprig. Found it. Spotted the tiny hole beneath it and crept forward. Briars tugged out clumps of fur, but none caught my skin.

Score one for rabbitdom.

Squashing the voice in the back of my head saying jumping down a black hole without knowing who or what waited for me down there was suicide, I flung my legs into an awkward frenzied gallop.

The urge to check on Rook was a twitch in my neck. I resisted. Barely.

Snuffling sounds blew moist breath down my back as I scraped and clawed my way deeper. A sharp yelp stung my ears—the hound's introduction to the briars. I crawled until the light behind me winked out and all was darkness. My eyesight had weakened as a rabbit, along with all my other senses as they were filtered through the skin.

Muted voices drifted up to me from far below me. The tone indicated curiosity more than fear. That heartened me. The púcas wouldn't recognize this skin as mine, but I hoped they would be willing to bargain for a bite to eat and a place to rest until Rook came for me. However long that took. Assuming he survived.

Please let him be alive.

The farther I went, the more I began wondering if I was alone in this section of the burrow. The hounds might have flushed the púcas farther into their tunnels than I was willing to go. Though I was safe for now, I knew the bramble hedge would thwart the beasts only long enough for them to realize that as shallow as this section of tunnel was, they could likely track me over ground until I emerged in an unprotected spot.

The longer I stayed, the harder I fought the inevitable and the greater risk I was to the púcas who dwelled here. They wouldn't welcome the discovery of their burrow by predators or its destruction.

I bargained with myself. If I encountered a resident, I would ask for food and temporary shelter. For news of Rook if they had any. They must have spies guarding the entrance. They might know how the fight ended. If no one came to usher me out or guide me in, then I would stumble in the dark until I found the way out on my own.

Rook mentioned returning to Autumn, but I didn't see the point unless he felt residents of Autumn were more sympathetic to my plight, which I doubted. Living in harmony with Winter, they must want Unseelie rule.

"Who are you?" The timid voice was absorbed by the damp walls.

Try as I might, I couldn't speak to answer him. Frustrated, I thumped my foot and hissed out an odd squeal. A sigh filled my ears. Faint shuffling as the púca edged nearer.

"You're doing it wrong." The voice gentled. "You can't speak in this form. No one can. You're going to have to give your skin a voice. Go on. Think it. Let magic speak for you. It's the only way."

Pick a voice? Think it? Crazy as it sounded, what did I have to lose? I focused the same as I did when willing magic into my palm, only this time I envisioned the memory of how my voice sounded to me. I would die before admitting it out loud, but I visualized it as a thought bubble forming over my head.

"I'm Macsen Sullivan's daughter," a voice similar to mine said.

"Ah. We were expecting you last night." More rustling sounds. "Come along. Follow me."

The púca led me through more twists and turns than I could ever keep straight on my own. If I had been myself, I could have followed our scent trails, but no way was two-legged me fitting down this rabbit hole.

Exhaustion tugged at the corners of my mind. The thought of losing my faint grip on this skin, of shifting to human while underground, made my mouth run dry.

That death would suck.

I clung to the hope the púca's offer of hospitality was genuine and that we would part as friends. If he had any more advice on how to make this body work for me, well, more's the better.

We crept through the tunnel for a half hour before light trickled in and illuminated my host. His fur was the same glossy black as all others of his kind. He was unremarkable except for one speck of white on his rump, like someone meant to give him a cotton tail but missed the mark.

"Watch your step," the púca cautioned before leaping out of sight.

Squinting against the bright light of the large cavern, I spotted my host and fumbled my jump to rejoin him. A few snickers made heat rise in my furry cheeks. Let them laugh. They had it easy. They were born shifters.

For me, experiencing my essence being stuffed into another form, one that retained phantom memories from its previous occupant, was downright creepy. Despite that, I was still kicking. I was fighting. So yuck it up, furballs. Laugh with me or at me, I didn't care. Not while being alive tasted so sweet.

My guide cleared his throat. "You'll be more comfortable in here."

Mustering my dignity, I sidestepped after him into a room large enough for a sitting human.

"In case of an accident," the púca answered my unasked question. "Stay here. We're all safer that way." The rabbit paused. "Your friend, Rook. If he arrives, I will send him to you. If he doesn't…"

"If he doesn't show up soon, I'll leave. I don't want to bring trouble to your door since you were kind enough to help me." I sat flat on my butt since my haunches were wobbly. "I haven't eaten in a long time. I'm running on fumes. If you had any food to share…" I couldn't say I would be grateful. That sounded too much like *thanks*, which might land me in hot water later, "…that would be nice."

The púca grinned. "We have plenty here. It's why we live on the border. Spring is flush with all sorts of delicacies, but Autumn is safer for our kind. Make yourself comfortable. I'll return shortly."

Following his advice, I forced my legs to work and flopped onto a bed of fresh straw. My paws ached and my muscles twinged. Everything hurt, but I shut my eyes with a smile. Pain meant I was still alive. It was hard to be upset about that.

CHAPTER TWENTY-FOUR

Straw crinkled beneath me when I twisted onto my back. Scratching an itchy spot on my belly with the short nails on my front paws, I yawned. My lids cracked open, and through the frame made of my hind legs, I saw him. Rook. His sleek head rested under his left wing.

Magic surged through me, snapping my grip on the skin. I screamed when it ripped free and I exploded to normal size, whacking the ceiling with my head.

"Freaking monkeys," I hissed.

Careful of the startled rook, I folded my legs and crammed myself into the smallest space possible to give us each breathing room. The bird stood pressed flush against the opposite wall, his tiny chest rising and falling rapidly.

"Sorry about that." I lifted the rabbit skin off my knee. "I wasn't expecting you."

He relaxed and cocked his head.

"I'm glad to see you. I was—" *don't say relieved,* "—relieved you're okay."

With a rustle of feathers, he lit on my knee.

"I guess you can't do the talking thing or you would have by now." I examined the tiny cubby, our sanctuary. "Did the food ever show up?" I felt around under my thighs. My fingers hit a bowl the size of my cupped palm. I raised it to my nose and inhaled, relieved as the sharp, sweet scent hit the back of my throat and revived my senses. "No idea what these are, but they smell delicious." I showed him one. "What do you think?"

His head tilted side to side while his beak worried the taut flesh. It was an odd-looking berry, deep-orange-colored flesh splattered with red splotches. He pierced the skin and ran his tongue over the tear.

When he tugged the oblong berry from my grasp and swallowed it whole, I figured that meant it was safe to eat as far as he could tell. Good enough for me. I picked one for myself and popped it into my mouth. Cool juices burst on my tongue, sweet, tart and delicious. I alternated feeding myself and Rook until he shook his head and hopped back to his corner while I polished off the rest and wiped my sticky fingers on the bedding.

While I sat there enjoying the sensation of having a full stomach, the bird vanished in a blast of magic. A heartbeat later, Rook's base form crammed the other half of the room, squishing me against the wall.

"We should talk." He grunted, shifting his weight while trying to cross his legs like mine.

"Hold still." I pulled his legs to either side of my hips, unhooked my ankles and straightened my legs above his lap until I could drape them over his thighs and brace them on the opposite wall. Tall as he was, Rook's head brushed the ceiling. He had to sit with his neck bent hard to one side. "Here. Wiggle down some. Not like that. You need to scoot your butt closer to me. There. Isn't that better?"

His eyes twinkled. "Much."

I glanced down at the meeting of our pelvises and slowly arched an eyebrow. "Glad to hear it."

His gaze swept over me. "Are you hurt?"

"I wasn't the one who faced down the hounds." I nudged his hip with the toe of my shoe. "Are you okay?"

A stiff roll of his shoulders was his answer.

Knowing better than to push, I changed strategies. "What's the plan?"

"We return to Autumn." He gave me no time to argue before adding, "Black Dog keeps a den there."

"Do you really believe if we find him that he's going to switch places with me?"

"Yes," he said. "I do."

"What makes you so sure?" If Mac viewed finding the king's killer more important than saving me, that's what he would do. The sense of justice that fueled his legend would settle for nothing less. The woods buzzed with news of the hunt. If Macsen wanted to play rescuer, he was missing his cue.

"You're his heir," Rook said, as though it should be obvious. "He will help if given the chance."

"If he's still in Faerie, he must have heard the rumors by now." I lifted my hands. "But I don't see him."

"It depends." He traced the curve of my ankle. "Seasons change on Earth. Some are mild, some are harsh. The thing they all have in common is they will pass. Seasons are static here. Portions of each season reflect the best and worst facets of each period. If your father is in the desert or the tundra, the message will be delayed if it reaches him at all." Rook studied a crack in the dirt by his cheek. "We just don't know."

I stole a moment to ensure my voice wouldn't quaver. "That means he's either in his den and he doesn't care whether I live or die, which wouldn't surprise me, or he's so far away he might as well not care because the odds of him reaching me before the hounds do…" I banged my skull against the wall. "Either way it's a no-win situation. Why bother? Why risk our necks when it doesn't matter?"

"It's the only chance you've got." He tapped my knee. "We don't have anything better to do."

"Nothing at all." I scuffed my shoe on the dirt wall. "Just try not to die. Horribly."

He slid his hand forward until he cupped my thigh. "You've been so brave."

"Necessity isn't bravery." If anything, all the running showed prudent cowardice.

"You could have refused to accept your father's role, his fate. You didn't." His other hand caressed the opposite thigh. "Knowing the endgame, you could have surrendered. You haven't. You're fighting. I admire that."

The higher his hands crept, the more possessive his grip became and the more certain I was that I ought to shut him down hard. Fast. Before this sexy fae led me astray and my family history repeated.

Instead of doing the smart thing, I found myself leaning forward while he did the same.

"Fighting to survive is instinct." The harder life came at you, the harder you had to punch it in the face.

"Why can't you accept a compliment?" He hauled my hips closer to his, and the motion rocked me back against the wall. "You even fight those."

"I'm not used to hearing them, except for the backhanded kind. They're hard to trust." Breathing became difficult when he bent over me, his face, his lips, so close to mine. "They're words. Easy to say even when you don't mean them."

He crowded my space until I had to flatten against the dirt wall if I wanted to escape him. The problem being I wasn't sure I did. In fact, I found myself reaching for him, drawn into him.

I ran the long strands of his hair through my fingers. "What are we doing?"

He covered my hand with his. "I'm hoping you will kiss me."

"You're a fan of short-term commitments, huh?" I teased. "Just like a guy."

"Thierry," he chastised me.

His breath fanned my cheeks. His lips parted. I almost tasted him.

"Wait." I pressed a finger to his mouth. "This won't count as consummating our marriage, will it?"

Rook's dark chuckle made me shiver. "If a kiss is your idea of consummation…"

"Ha. Try to turn it around on me." I slid my hand across his cheek, his skin warm silk under my fingers. "I seem to recall being tricked into a marriage I still, quite frankly, question the validity of. I just want to make sure that if I actually let you kiss me, that it's not some kind of binding spit-swapping contract I can't break later."

If I had a later.

"I warned you." His skin flushed. "Trust I will keep you safe. As to the rest…"

"I can't help trusting you a teeny-tiny bit when you keep saving me. I know I shouldn't. You're working an angle. If I only knew—"

His mouth lowered to mine, silencing my doubts, filling my head with his smoky taste.

He gripped the leather straps on my shoulders and brought me flush against him. Roots tangled in my hair and dust sprinkled onto my lashes. His tongue slipped between my lips, and I sighed against him.

Rook was attempting to drag me under him, without much resistance, when a small throat cleared.

"Forgive the intrusion. The hounds. They breached the easternmost tunnel. Our little ones room not far from there. We evacuated the babes in time," he added hastily, "but you both must go. Please."

"Of course." I disentangled the best I could from Rook. "Which way out is safest?"

"We must return to Autumn." Rook hummed. "Is the western tunnel clear?"

"As far as I know." The púca's whiskers twitched. "We'll send a scout to see you on your way."

"That is very kind of you." Rook eased his hand under my ass and dragged out a rumpled rabbit skin. "If you could give us privacy while we shift? Once we're ready, we'll join you at the junction."

After a slight hesitation, the púca bobbed its head. "That's fair, but be quick."

Once our host left, Rook offered me the skin. "Do you think you can manage a while longer?"

"I think so." I dusted the soft fur. "I got a nap before you arrived, and I've eaten. All in all, I feel better now than I have since we left Mom's house. Did you come all the way down here in rook form?"

He nodded. "The rook in me hates being unable to see sky." His gaze rolled over our surroundings and a shudder rippled through him. "Try to keep up."

"That sounds like a challenge." Had everyone noticed my lack of hopping skills?

"We can race if you like." His eyes twinkled. "To the victor go the spoils."

A trap if I ever heard one. "How exactly does the victor think he's getting spoiled?"

Rook bent over me. "I will allow you to make payments toward my winnings."

I pulled him down to me and nipped his bottom lip. "How gracious of you."

"One kiss now..." His mouth brushed mine. "After I win, you owe me ninety-nine more."

"It's a deal." I stuck out my hand, and he shook it. "Now, give me some room."

He retreated to his corner where he slid into his other form like a letter into an envelope. The bird that was Rook cawed.

"I'm going as fast as I can." I pushed myself upright and placed the skin on my head, tugging the twin holes over my eyes and peering through the slashes.

Calm. I had to get calm. Ignore Rook. Forget Mom. Shaw— don't even go there. All those things got shoved into the farthest corner of my mind.

Skin tightening, I felt when the pelt latched on to me. Remembered sensations swamped me. Grass tickling the sensitive pads of my feet. The crisp bite of fresh vegetation. Warm sun on soft fur. Scattered impressions rose to the surface of my mind and tugged me under their spell. Magic quivered over my flesh, folding my essence onto itself, stacking me neatly inside the pelt.

With a nod to me, the Rook hopped from our room through the short tunnel into a four-way intersection.

It took me longer to acclimate, but I managed. Both the rook and the púca appeared surprised to see me so soon, which grated. Lucky for them, the worst I could manage was wriggling my cute button nose at them.

If birds could smirk, that damn bird was shooting one right at me.

"We're ready." I used magic to carry my voice and prove my superiority over Mute McSmirkypants. "Let's go."

The púca darted down a tunnel before the words were out of my mouth—mind? I couldn't blame him. We had endangered his home and family. I just hoped by leaving that Rook and I hadn't jumped out of the frying pan and into the fire.

CHAPTER TWENTY-FIVE

"This is as far as I go." The púca worried his front paws together. "Once you have left, I will tell the hunt you're no longer our guests. The rules of hospitality apply. I won't tell them where you've gone." He bowed before me. "Your sacrifice will be remembered. You are *dlúthchara* to me and mine."

I ran the Irish Gaelic word through my memory and came up with *close friend.*

"You do me an honor." I returned the gesture. "We part as friends."

Contorting his lithe body, the púca vanished into the safety of the burrow.

Rook hopped toward the tunnel's opening, dug his talons into the soft dirt and leapt for the sky. Decaying leaves, wood smoke and cloves hit my nose. We were back in Autumn. The rabbit skin dampened the rest. Until I reached the outside or I shed this form, I was stuck receiving sensory information through a filter, which sucked. This was a lesson in putting my other senses to work. I was too dependent on my nose.

After a while, the rook popped its head back into the hole and then flapped its wings. Message received. I exited the burrow, cautious of those first steps into sunlight.

Magic brushed against my shoulder, and Rook stood beside me. After some false starts, I got the rabbit skin removed and shifted back to good old two-legged me. That first lungful of fresh air made me giddy, and stretching felt divine. Pops shuddered down my spine as I reached my arms over my head.

"We can't risk being out in the open." He sounded sorry to interrupt.

"I know." I scooped the pelt off the ground, dusting it before I rolled it up and shoved it into a pouch in the armor covering my thigh. "Ready."

He set off down a narrow trail marked by clumps of iridescent mushrooms reflecting the sunlight, and I followed a few steps behind. The path smelled familiar, but I sniffed, certain we had never gone this way.

My slower pace gave me a prime view of his backside, not that I was complaining, but it raised some questions I ought to ask. Like why the fabric of his cloak and armor were torn but his skin was smooth underneath. Did he heal fast like me? Was it a byproduct of shifting? Was that how his broken arm reset?

Even better—where did our clothes go when we changed shape? Did they always return the same way? If I scuffed my shoes, shifted, then shifted back, would the shoes still be scuffed? I pulled a weary hand down my face. The answer was an obvious *yes* because Rook's leather armor resembled a rawhide chew toy, allowing me glimpses of flexing muscle in his back as he walked.

Pale skin I shouldn't be admiring.

That kiss... It changed things, and I wasn't sure what came next. Out here, I wasn't safe and warm or fed and comfortable. Out here, I was exposed and afraid. That kiss, no matter how nice it had been, wasn't as important as exploring my slim survival options.

"According to the information I gleaned in court, Black Dog's den isn't too far from here."

My gaze lifted to peg the back of his head. "You mean you've never been?"

"He doesn't welcome visitors." He glanced back. "He avoids favoring either side by befriending neither. Or so the rumors say." He kept moving. "It's said loneliness is what drove him to the mortal realm, where he could take a lover who wouldn't compromise his honor, and there he met your mother."

A sliver of apprehension worked its way under my skin. Black Dog was legendary. He was also critical to maintaining balance in Faerie, so his exploits would make for juicy gossip at court. People—especially fae—loved hearing their peers were as flawed as they were. It validated their choices and made them feel better about all the naughty things they did and hoped remained a secret.

But Rook was so well versed, it brought all my doubts bubbling to the surface. Not that it did me any good. He was my lifeline, even if I wasn't sure where he was anchored.

I finger combed my hair and freshened my braid. "How long do you think before the púcas break the news?"

"Not long." Tension hung around his shoulders. "It's not much farther now."

Resolved to see this through, I let him guide me while I noted landmarks in case I needed to find my way back out alone. My nose also made critical notations. The air went from crisp and clear to smelling of pungent markers that reeked of warning. Urine. Buckets of it. Some of it old, but most of it fresh.

Nice, Dad. Real nice.

Sneezing, I wiped my tickling nose. "What types of predators are in the area?"

He laughed. Out loud. At me.

"Dumb question," I allowed. "I smell two distinct scent markers. One is fresher than the other."

Rook stopped and scanned the area. "Your father?"

"I don't think so." I rubbed my nose. "It almost reminds me of…"

"Get down," he snapped.

My hand shot to my glove, lips moving on my Word. Rook sank his shoulder into my gut, tackling me to the ground as a fluorescent-yellow blur bolted past.

While I lay panting underneath him, an earsplitting roar had me yanking my hand free of my glove and powering up my runes. Rook's eyes narrowed beyond me. I tilted my head back and, in the upside-down world, spotted a fluorescent-yellow panther-like thing. Its color hurt my sensitive eyes, but not as much as its saber teeth would if I let it get hold of me. I bucked my hips to unseat Rook, but I was stuck until he let me go.

His immunity to my primary defense mechanism was a pain in my ass.

"You dare enter these woods," a rumbling voice challenged.

It was easier to ask Rook, so I did. "Tell me the cat isn't talking."

"Hush, Thierry." He lifted his hands. "We mean you no harm. We only seek the Black Dog."

"Ha." The great cat chuckled. "You are a bird. Food. What can food do to me?"

"I am the Morrigan's son," he said with an edge.

"I know who you are, bastard son of Gregory the Smith." The cat spat, "You will leave. Now."

Rook's face mottled. "Don't speak my father's name. You don't have that right."

A vicious snarl lifted the cat's lip. "You dare enter these woods with that child and speak of rights?"

Deciding the cat wasn't going to pounce just yet, I tilted my head back again. "I'm not a child."

"I have known you since before your feet touched mortal soil. You are a babe to one such as me. You are welcome on your father's land, in his home, always, Thierry Thackeray." His grin bared too many teeth to be what I considered friendly. "You may stay, but the Morrigan's hatchling must go."

"Rook is my guardian." I kept calm while my insides quivered. "He is my *coimirceoir*."

The big cat hissed at Rook. "Who granted you that privilege?"

"The Huntsman." A cruel twist of his lips turned my stomach. "She is my wife by common fae law."

That thick tail started twitching. "What do you say to that, girl?"

I bit my cheek before answering. "The Faerie High Court recognized his claim."

Closing its dark green eyes, the cat sighed. "Child, how you try me."

I shoved Rook off me and rolled over to face the cat. "Sorry?"

Its toes began drumming its claws into the ground. "Did you not hear my warnings?"

"You sent the pixie?" I shoved into a kneeling position. "That was you in the shower?"

The great cat shuddered nose to tail. "So much water…"

"I'm not flexible enough for the alternative," I said dryly. "My tongue's on the short side too."

The strangled sound must have come from Rook, because the cat eyed me with genuine pity.

"I aimed to preserve your privacy and indulged my own…aversions…at your expense. That was an unforgivable oversight. I did hope the birds on your mother's lawn would suffice. Failing that, the feather I left on her pillow. I hoped you would read its warning—" his eyes narrowed on Rook, "—and avoid him at all costs."

"The feather was another warning?" My lip curled, and I growled at Rook. "You said the etchings were coordinates to Faerie."

"I had to bring you here." His shoulders straightened. "When I realized you couldn't read the runes, I took advantage."

"You? Take advantage?" I scoffed. "There's a shocker."

The cat twitched his tail.

"The warnings didn't help because I didn't know who Rook was. I thought he—" I jabbed a finger at my sulky husband, "—was Raven. The chess lingo flew right over my head."

With a huff, the cat shook his head. "I see now I should have stayed to make you understand, but I did not wish to alarm you by appearing in person." He rolled his shoulders. "Some find me intimidating. I did not wish you to be afraid."

"Afraid isn't the word I would use." Terrified sounded about right.

His rusty chuckle coaxed a timid smile from me. "Of course not."

"Since we're old pals, is there something I can call you?"

"I will give you my Name when there are not as many sharp ears around." His eyes narrowed on Rook before turning back to me. "I have heard of your trials and am sorry for them. As recompense, I am yours to call. You are mine to protect. If you require me, you have only to summon me. Until such time as we are able to speak freely—" another cutting glare sliced through Rook, "—you may call me Diode."

Rook shifted closer to me, causing Diode's lips to quiver. I elbowed him hard in the ribs.

"Well, Diode, we have a problem." I exhaled. "I don't suppose my father is around?"

His lips mashed together. His tail thumped harder. With effort, he shook his head.

"Are you okay?" The air rippled with the scent of a triggered enchantment.

Diode took a moment to loosen his jaw before answering. "Yes."

I studied him. "What type of spell was that?"

"Noticed, did you?" He purred with amusement. "I was charmed—of my own free will—by your father. I never had occasion to regret that decision until now. I apologize, but I cannot tell you where he is. It is physically impossible—" His head snapped up. "The hunt comes. Hurry. Follow me."

Rook rolled onto his feet and offered me his hand.

I exchanged a worried glance with him.

"All is not lost," he assured me. "If Black Dog was standing behind you, Diode couldn't point."

The big cat leapt ahead and called to us. "The entrance is hidden, but those hounds know your father well. It's only a matter of time before they locate his den. I'll do what I can to help until then."

We bolted after him, struggling to match his lengthy stride.

"Dim-witted beasts," Diode muttered. "True hunters would run alone. Not run in a pack."

What a catty sentiment. "Is Macsen dim-witted?"

"Since you haven't met him," he said on a huff, "I won't shatter your illusions."

My side twinged when I laughed.

Our run was brief. Diode charged an enormous tree that would rival a redwood back home. He hunched his shoulders and pawed at the base. The rest I couldn't see. I glanced at Rook, who studied the area, the wide tree and the method of entry much the same as I did. My attention on him spread a smug grin across his face.

A soft click brought my focus back to Diode and the tree. A three-foot section of its trunk swung open, and the cat leaned against the door to keep it wedged open. He craned his neck, ears twitching.

"Get inside." Diode batted me with his paw. "Hurry."

I cuffed Rook by the wrist and dragged him into the gloomy chamber behind me. Diode ducked inside, and the door sealed on his heels.

"That will hold them a while." Smugness dripped from Diode's words. "Follow me."

He hip-bumped Rook, flattening him against the entry's wall. Me he urged forward with a flick of his tail. I didn't check my hubby for boo-boos. I drifted into the circular room and shut my eyes, inhaling the rich scent of tobacco smoke and parchment. Fresh scents. Like I had just missed Mac.

I had inherited my office at the conclave from my father. It used to smell this way, like him. I still caught the phantom scent when I cracked open his reference books. I strolled the perimeter of the room, examining his floor-to-ceiling shelves, afraid to touch the delicate wood carvings lining his walls but unable to tear myself away from perusing the motley collection of knickknacks and books that added up to who my father was.

I pulled up short when I caught Diode's sad expression.

"He never wanted this," the great cat said.

Before I could ask what *this* was—me or Mom or this whole situation—the entire room began trembling. Baubles tumbled from the shelves and crashed onto the floor.

"What is that?" I saved a tiny owl shaken from its ledge on reflex.

"The hunt." Diode's fur stood on end. "They won't stop until they knock down the door."

Rook came to my side. "How long does that give us?"

"A half hour." The cat hissed in response. "Perhaps less."

Rook's lips thinned. "Do we have your permission to search the den?"

Diode tore his narrowed gaze from Rook and nodded at me. "She may do as she pleases. You may stay where you are if you value your tail feathers."

Crossing his arms over his chest, Rook stood back and entered a staring contest with the cat.

I had a good idea who was going to win, paws down.

"Okay." I dusted my hands. "Here we go."

Despite my first impression, and the fact the entire den fit inside a hollow tree, the central room was a good twenty feet in circumference. Fae magic at work. Making room where there was none.

Opening a door across from the entryway, I stepped down a long hall lit by hand-blown mason jars hung by cords from the ceiling. They were filled with—I squinted up at one—pissed-off pixies.

Well, that explained the second warning I had received about Rook. Apparently, the petite fae were light sources and messengers all rolled into one easy-to-capture package. They were probably willing to do anything for their freedom.

I counted seven jars as I passed under them. There must have been twice as many doors. I tried one after the other, but each one was locked. Great. Tell me to look where I please but ensure I got nowhere. Whoever or whatever lurked behind those doors stayed off-limits to me.

Giving up on the stealth approach, I called, "Macsen?"

No answer.

"Macsen Sullivan?" I reached the end of the hall and the final door. "Black Dog?"

Nothing.

Gripping the knob, I turned the handle and—to my surprise—the door opened. Right onto a wall of solid dirt. A hall full of doors that led nowhere. Unless.... Why keep all those pixies if their light was never used? Macsen could be using the area for storing them, but sharp doubts prodded me.

Murmuring my Word, I removed my glove and lit up that hand. Closing my eyes, I blocked out the thudding behind me, the tremors under my feet. I filled my lungs with air from the hall, sorting a whiff of Diode and discarding it to focus on the tobacco aroma. Once I had it, I followed the scent to a nondescript door on the right. Certain I was on to something, I gripped the knob with my left hand.

Subtle warmth spread from my palm, up my arm, to wrap me in its embrace. Once the magic dispersed, I opened the door, wary of what awaited me. Annoyed chattering reached my ears first. Another set of jars filled with angry pixies made the inner room glow.

I stepped inside, drawn to a battered desk in the corner. More bookshelves lined these walls. Modern bindings crammed between ancient tomes. Printed reports were pinned down by a glass inkwell. An old comic book wrapped in plastic sat beside an empty mug.

This must be Macsen's home office. Judging by his chaotic filing system, not much had changed since he last occupied the space I inherited from him at the marshal's office. I grinned when I spotted his sleek coffee maker and a bag of dark roast beans. Faerie wasn't wired for electricity. He brewed with magic or he didn't drink. I could admire the man's dedication to remaining caffeinated.

"Macsen?" I glanced over my shoulder and wet my lips. "Dad?"

I held my breath. Nothing. He wasn't here.

"Why am I not surprised?" I turned a slow circle. "You're never around when I need you."

The ground under my feet shook. I had to go. Now. Before the hunt trapped me in the den. Part of me thought dying here would serve my father right. It would definitely get his attention if he spent days scrubbing my blood from the threadbare rug in the hall. Assuming he didn't toss it away like he had discarded me. The rest of me wanted to keep living more than I wanted to exact some kind of twisted and petty revenge death.

Death was pretty much the opposite outcome I was hoping for.

CHAPTER TWENTY-SIX

The pixies under glass got one last look from me before I headed back down the hall toward the main room. I didn't have the heart to search the rest of the den. What was the point? If my father had been here and heard us tromping around his house, he would have put in an appearance by this point.

That no one had jumped out or yelled *get off my lawn* told me Black Dog wasn't in residence. My final hope extinguished. It was me versus the hounds now. No one could save me but myself.

Diode's furious scream urged my feet into a run. I grasped the doorknob and held on as the den rattled. When the tremors settled, I flung open the door in time to watch the first hound leap through the opening they had made. Others poured through after it, filling the room with snarling, yapping dogs.

Rook and Diode were nowhere in sight.

The first hound's nostrils flared. He swung his head, saw me and charged.

Too slow. Shock had numbed my reflexes.

They had left me. *Rook left me.*

The dog's shoulder hit the door and flung me back against the wall. It skidded, snarling and snapping into the hall with me. From the corner of my eye, I spotted the others noticing what had happened and running full force at me with their teeth gleaming.

I slammed the door shut and grasped the handle with my left hand, willing enough magic into it to, I hoped, fuse the metal and buy me a few minutes. A low snarl jerked me around, and I flattened against the door. As growls rose in eager chorus behind me, the hound in front of me licked his muzzle.

He could have been any of them, but I got the sinking feeling he was Raven and that I was truly caught. His eyes gave him away. They were twin voids, black, eternal and shimmering with emotion and experiences too complex for me to untangle at a glance. They reminded me of Rook's before I knew him better.

"Nice doggy." I lifted my hands. "You don't want to—"

He lunged. I ducked and rolled under him, pushing to my feet to brace for his next charge. Raven leapt for my throat. *Kill or be killed.* I shoved my hands out in front to deflect him and ended up clutching a fistful of fur. His teeth snapped an inch from my nose. Hot spittle flew in my face.

My left palm flooded with all the energy I could syphon in those split seconds, and I fed it to him.

Raven's back bowed. He yelped and tried to backpedal. Too late. Magic grabbed him, and it wasn't letting go. Power seeped under his skin, lifting his fur on end. Deeper and deeper it plumbed.

The hounds were soul catchers covered in fur. They were hollow, unthinking beasts who lived for the thrill of bringing down prey and pleasing their master, filling that aching emptiness. This hound wasn't like that.

His soul burned white hot and sizzled wherever tendrils of my magic brushed against it. Oh yes. This was Raven. This was old magic, an old soul, and it hadn't lived this long by yielding in battle.

The wood at my back thumped as bodies smacked it. If they burst through, it was over. Staring into Raven's cold eyes made me wonder if it wasn't already.

Drawing magic up from my toes, through my body and into my fingertips, I slammed every last drop of power I had left into him. His body seized. His heart stuttered. Before he recovered, I guided my energy there, let it encase the struggling organ, and then I ripped with all my might. I tugged and pulled him magically while our physical bodies remained locked in place with his teeth at my throat.

His snarling choked to a whine. Shock rounded his eyes the instant before his soul flickered and snuffed, suffusing my limbs with so much power I vibrated with my heady newfound strength. With morbid pleasure, I skinned Raven.

One minute I held the hound by its throat, the next I clutched a slab of meat.

For once, I didn't feel a twinge of remorse. No sympathetic pain, either. Raven would have killed me. I just beat him to it. No doubt I would pay for his death. Later. Right now I was alive, and that's all that mattered. *Be grateful and keep moving.*

The room behind me fell silent. The door stopped thumping. A mournful symphony filled my ears, burning the back of my throat from the force of my instinctual desire to join in their grieving. But I wasn't sad. Not for Raven. I was exhilarated. High on the essence of the purest concentration I had ever tasted.

I almost wished Shaw was here to bleed off the excess as he had with O'Shea, as he had dozens of times before that. But as I eyed the door, a foreign confidence whispered through my blood.

We can take them all, make them pay for their trespass, make them regret ever coming for you or yours. Let me make them hurt.

I swallowed hard. That voice wasn't mine, even if the sentiment was tempting.

With my head clearing, I spared a queasy peek at the remains gripped in my left hand. Shudders wracked me as I forced myself to look at what I had done. Either Faerie was giving my powers a boost or maybe being in my father's home, a place covered in his magical residue, was to blame for it. I wasn't sure.

Unable to stomach holding on any longer, I loosened my grip and let the hound's corpse fall to the floor. Its thick pelt draped over my feet. I kicked it aside, made it a half-dozen steps toward the office, before I turned.

Skins were power. I knew that now. The hound—the *prince*—was dead. He had no more use for his fur. His pelt might as well be put to good use. I darted back, snatched up the skin and hesitated.

Either I hadn't noticed or hadn't had the juice before to sense the subtle magic coating each doorknob. Now their static hums drifted inside my range of hearing.

I reached for the closest one as the door behind me exploded in iron hardware and splinters. No fate beyond its threshold could be worse than what waited for me here. I opened the door and ran inside. No. *Outside*. I recognized the insect chorus and the hazy quality of the air. I was back in Spring.

I spun around in the clearing. No hint of the den or trace of magic lingered. The best I could hope for was that the hounds lacked the power to operate the door or that it sealed after I tumbled through.

This explained a whole hell of a lot. I always wondered how one person could play peacekeeper across an entire realm. Impossible. Like Santa Claus. One person couldn't service the needs of an entire world. Well, I stood corrected. The hall leading to Macsen's office was riddled with doors. Who knew where all of them led? One to every season was a given, but one to each house? What an amazing secret he kept.

Okay. So. New plan. Rook was missing. Diode had vanished. One prince was dead.

One prince was dead.

There was a clear winner. Would that end the hunt? Or must the victor kill the tribute? I had no one to ask, no way to know, but I was betting my life and I wagered on *yes*.

I stood there with a skin in my fist and made a decision. Maybe it was the high thrumming through my veins or the fresh blood on my hands, but I wasn't running again. I was done with this game. My mom didn't deserve this. Neither did I. The one person who probably did was noticeably absent.

Instead of making use of my head start, I found a spot where a tree rooted beside a boulder, and I plopped down with my back resting on the moss-encrusted trunk, protected on two sides with a clear view ahead, and waited for the remaining hounds to find me. When they did, I would be ready.

My stomach grumbled about being empty. It seemed like ages since I fed Rook berries. Rook, who had abandoned me to face the hunt alone. That I could almost understand. Forgive? No. But he kept telling me not to trust him. He told me to believe the worst of him. Had I? Nope. I just carved out my heart and offered it up to him on a platter. I believed he was my friend. I thought he felt...something.

Clearly, I had sniffed one too many toadstools.

Diode's disappearance worried me more. I didn't know him, didn't know for sure he was telling the truth any more then Rook was, but he struck me as sincere, and he had led me to my father's den. I hoped he was safe wherever he was. I wished we could have talked more. I had so many questions.

"I wish Diode was here now," I said on an exhale.

Chills coasted over my nape. Instinct guided my eyes toward the lush green jungle-like interior where two eyes blinked out at me. Watchers.

Howls carried to my ears. It looked like the gang was all here. It might have been my imagination, but I read condemnation in the glittering red eye. I had cost the Unseelie their prince. The best-case scenario was yet another century-long Seelie reign.

Not my problem. Balancing justice in Faerie? That was Macsen's shtick, and he shouldn't have left me to wield it. It turned out I was afraid. Brief as my lifespan might be, I wanted every second, every minute, every hour of every day. If the Seelie hound bested me, then so be it. But he had a fight on his paws.

I stood and braced my feet apart. I hadn't bothered with my glove after leaving the den. I flexed my fingers and shook magic into their tips, frowning when the runes cast emerald light. The darker, colder glow worried me, but not enough I wouldn't use whatever the Unseelie prince's essence had left me for this final battle.

The thunder of eleven hounds' paws—ten more than I could take down at once—filled me with dread. I clutched the Unseelie prince's hide in my right hand so they could see I meant business.

The rules had always been the same for them.

This time they were in for a surprise.

The beasts galloped into the clearing then tapered their gait while studying me. Confusion knit their brows. They snuffled the air and looked to their leader, the tallest of them, the remaining prince.

That hound stepped forward, bowed his head and met my gaze. His was clear and untroubled. It wasn't confidence that he would win, though he seemed unafraid of losing, it was a calm acceptance. He swished his tail, and the beasts to either of his sides charged.

Okay, so not acceptance. He was going to hurl the others at me until I tired enough he could defeat me or until I blazed through them and he had to either face me or brand himself as a coward.

Drawing power into my left hand, I wished I had more than a pelt in the right. Intimidation hadn't worked. All it had done was show the Seelie prince I wasn't going down easy and allowed him time to cobble together a plan to wear me down. Not my smartest strategy yet, but the skin might come in handy.

If the rabbit skin retained memories of its former occupant, this skin might too. With the imprint fresh, it might shorten the learning curve from two to four legs.

Seconds before impact, the hounds yelped in panic, sliding when they tried to backpedal.

I darted a quick glance around the clearing while my nape prickled. "What the…?"

Their gazes fixated on a point behind me. I slowly turned my head and spotted a retina-singeing blur of neon fur and saber teeth land in a menacing crouch on the cold gray slab of stone at my back. A fast grin stretched my cheeks. It felt so damn good to have someone in my corner, to not be alone.

I crept closer to Diode, keeping my eyes on the hounds as they retreated back to their prince. "Come to watch the show?"

"I am not much for spectator sports," Diode purred. "Might I be of assistance?"

My heart tumbled. "Is that—allowed?"

"Asks the girl clutching the pelt of a prince?" His laughter rumbled. "All bets are off."

"Don't stick out your neck on my account." I lifted my chin. "I can handle this."

"I have broken so many rules." His muzzle bumped my shoulder. "What is one more?"

I leaned against him. "I'm glad you're here."

"I wish your father could have been here." His sandpaper tongue rasped over my cheek.

"Would it have worked?" I had to ask. "Could he have swapped places with me?"

"No." Diode huffed. "Once you accepted the terms, you were bound by them."

"I figured." I wet my lips. "Do you know...? I mean, I came back and you were both gone."

"I have not seen Rook since we parted ways outside the den." He flicked his ears. "If I had not known you were Macsen's daughter, I would have when his doors opened for you. They answer to no one else. When the hounds breached the den, I led Rook out another exit near Winter. I trusted you would find your own way out. I see my faith was not misplaced. Macsen would be proud."

I shrugged off his compliment, even as it warmed me. "How did you find me?"

"I heard your call." He sniffed. "Did I not say I would always come when summoned?"

"Not a sentiment I would expect to hear from a cat," I teased.

"Hmph." He swished his tail. "Perhaps your father rubbed off on me after all."

The shock of seeing Diode must have faded. The prince snarled at the defectors, snapping at the nearest dog and biting off his ear. The others whined softly and backed away from him, toward us. Once out of range of the prince's jaws, their nails dug into the shredded ground. Their mouths fell open on deep barks the others were quick to encourage.

"I will handle the whelps." Diode revved up his purring. "You take down the prince."

Claws raked across stone when the cat leapt over my head and hit the grass running. He collided with the first hound, knocking it backward with a yelp while ripping out the other's throat. He turned to his second kill, and I stepped away from the safety of the boulder, raised my left hand and waved.

"Let's end this," I called to the prince.

His paw stomped, and another set of hounds charged.

Diode intercepted, gutting them with a swipe of his claws.

"We can do this all day." I gestured toward the cat. "He hasn't broken a sweat."

Shrinking against the prince, the remaining hounds whined. He snapped at them and shoved them out of his way with his shoulders. A steady grumble poured out his throat as he left the safety of the pack. He cut his eyes toward Diode, the question in them clear.

"He won't fight this battle for me." I lifted the Unseelie prince's pelt. "He doesn't have to."

The Seelie prince's eyes lit on that swath of fur then flicked to me. I guess he wasn't impressed. Instead of meeting me halfway, he threw back his head and howled until the hounds behind him stopped trembling and meekly came to his sides.

Back to square one. They far outnumbered us. Even Diode couldn't tackle all of them at once, and I couldn't focus on the prince while the others gnawed on me.

This time four hounds loped forward, hesitant but determined.

"Shift," a bold voice commanded. "The others won't kill one of their own."

Rook.

He was here.

Gripping the skin tighter, I pulled it over my head and looked at the world through a dog's eyes.

Change came faster this time, fueled by fear and adrenaline. As magic shrank me to fit the container I had chosen, I managed two wobbling steps. Before the first hounds reached me, they pulled up short. Two ventured hesitant wags of their tails. They chuffed, sounds the skin knew how to mimic, then snuffled me from nose to ass.

Mostly my ass. Seriously. Cold wet nose pressed to my... Never mind. Moving on.

Swishing my tail, I hoped to send a *hi guys* message while I swatted them away from my rear.

When the press of bodies cleared, I noticed the prince stood where I saw him last.

Coward. I let anger rumble up the back of my throat.

The dogs beside me stiffened and jerked their heads toward him. They glanced between us, and for a heartbeat I thought they might turn on me. Instead, they slicked their ears back and trotted out in front. *Thank you, Rook.* Between the pelt and the Unseelie prince's essence still tingling under my skin, I must have passed the test. Packs followed the dominant hunter, and it looked like I was it.

The princes may have oozed entitlement, but I was Black Dog's daughter. In a way, I was pack. He had been plucked from the Huntsman's favorites. Technically, some of these dogs might be aunts or uncles of mine. I crushed that thought before it made me sentimental. I couldn't afford a soft spot. Not while the bloodthirsty beasts at my sides waited for me to call the shots. To end yet another life.

Relying on the skin's memory to form the right vocals, I ordered the pack to circle wide and pin the prince in case he bolted. I was done playing nice. This ended now. No do-overs or take-backs. All or nothing.

"Let the skin do the work," Rook called.

I flexed my paws, felt my nails rake the damp earth. I filled my lungs and listened to my heart as it pumped hard and fast. This skin fit me better than the other. This one craved the wash of blood and the splinter of bone between my teeth, and I gave myself over to those hungers. I let wildness infuse my blood, allowed one prince's essence, his hatred for the opposing house, to saturate my senses and fuel the bloodcurdling howl ripping out of my throat. I tore up the ground launching myself forward.

The other hounds vanished into the underbrush, little more than shadows with night falling fast. My blood sang with the fading light. No wonder Unseelie preferred the dark if this was her potent call.

The Seelie prince darted glances around the clearing. His soft whines attempted to lure others to his cause, but they were loyal to me. They were *mine.* I called encouragement and whipped them into a frenzy. One or two rushed in to snap at the prince's tail. He spun and gnashed his teeth at them.

Chicken. Too afraid to face me. Too proud to run. He stood his ground and braced for attack.

Twisting away from his teeth, I slammed my shoulder against his side, bit down where his throat had been and tasted air. He swung his skull, crashing into mine, and I saw stars. I stumbled away and shook my head—then really, really wished I hadn't done that. While I was blinking away vertigo, he nipped my side. It *hurt*. I danced out of range and started doubting Rook's advice.

I had the power to end the Seelie, to finish this, but I couldn't tap into that wellspring of princely energy now. Even if I could, my magic required rune-to-skin contact. Thanks to the thick fur coating me, that was impossible. But if I risked shifting back now, he could snap my slender human neck or rip open my delicate stomach.

One of the hounds chomped on the prince's tail and dragged him howling back a few paces before returning to his post. I might have felt bad for the prince if he hadn't used the same tactics on me.

Before he regained his focus, I dug my nails in deep and sprang for his throat. My teeth sank in his fur and found purchase in his skin. I bit down harder, flinging my head from side to side until the tang of iron filled my mouth. The prince struggled and snapped at me. He clawed and kicked me, but he couldn't break my hold. While my stomach roiled, I gnawed on him until the predator in me was satisfied I had done my job.

When he ceased struggling, I loosened my jaw and let him slump to the ground in a ragged heap of bloody fur. His eyes fogged over as I stood there, licking my muzzle.

The eyes in the forest converged on me. When the red-eyed one spoke, his voice came from no mouth I could see, and I shuddered.

No wonder they kept to the shadows.

"You have killed the Unseelie prince." He glanced to the Watcher on his right. That one nodded. "You have also slayed the Seelie prince." Their voices layered together. "This is not the outcome we foresaw. You must accompany us to Summer, where the High Court will review our accountings."

I lowered my head and sent magic coasting through my limbs. The skin fell away and left me with blood turning my cheeks sticky. I knelt there on the ground until I could breathe without gagging, then snagged the pelt and shoved to my feet. I should have left the skin there. I could have tossed it onto the other prince and been done with both of them, but a niggling doubt cautioned me to keep hold of it, at least until I spoke with the High Court.

My legs were rubber. I was grateful when Diode prowled over to me in a show of support. Rook put an arm around my waist and pressed a brief kiss to my temple. The knuckles of his other hand brushed over the pelt.

I flinched at his gentle touch. "I'm sorry about your brother."

I had no choice, but Rook knew that. He wasn't blaming me, which somehow made it worse.

"I am too," he managed, voice thick with emotion. "If you like, I can put this somewhere safe, until you need it."

"All right." I handed it to him, feeling like a pallbearer passing over her charge.

Together the three of us faced the Watchers. Something told me we had a long night ahead of us.

CHAPTER TWENTY-SEVEN

Crossing into Summer was like stepping onto the back porch of my mother's house in August. The sky was clear, the night clean. A fat moon hung overhead, and stars glittered as far as I could see. Frog song carried, accompanied by a bawdy cricket chorus and the bass hooting of something I felt safe assuming wasn't an owl. Still, more than anywhere else in Faerie, this place reminded me of home.

"How much farther is it?" I wasn't in any hurry to face down the consuls, I was just curious.

Distances seemed oddly fluid here. Almost as if by wanting to be somewhere, I got there faster. Considering how this sweat-sticky procession dragged, I began believing the opposite must also be true.

Diode butted his head against my thigh. "Not much longer now."

I glanced at Rook, whose arm still hung around my waist and whose fingers rubbed my hip. His eyes were distant, the rest of his features arranged in such a way as to discourage conversation.

Since talking wasn't an option, I settled for scratching Diode behind his ears. His rumbling purr thanked me. The sound was soothing. Odd, since I wasn't a cat person.

While I mulled over the day's events, our group strolled from a perfect summer night into a humid morning that promised midday would be a scorcher. The kind of day where, if there had been a sidewalk, you could have fried eggs on it then crisped yourself two strips of bacon.

"We have arrived," the Watchers announced together.

I examined our surroundings. "Where are the Halls of Summer?"

They pointed toward a dark splotch in the landscape.

"What is that?" I squinted at it.

"The way in," Rook answered.

After remaining quiet for so long, his voice startled me.

"The Halls of Summer are in a swimming hole." I shook my head. "Of course they are."

As our party approached the entrance, I could see it was, in fact, a natural pond. It reminded me of a case Shaw and I had worked together.

A farmer went to water his cows one day and found them standing in the middle of his field around a pond, measuring twelve feet in diameter, that hadn't been there the night before. Sinkholes are common in Texas. Underground springs are too, so the farmer didn't think much of it.

Word spread and local teens started sneaking onto his property to swim at Blue Hole, so named because the water was Caribbean blue and clear as the purest spring water. So clear you could have seen the bottom if there had been one, but the hole seemed to go on forever. Which became the topic of debate between the farmer, the geologists interested in studying the phenomenon, and the teens who figured the fastest way to figure out what was down there was to dive for it. And dive they did.

But they didn't come back.

When the tally shot to five missing teens, the conclave caught wind of it and sent us to investigate. Turned out to be freshwater mermaids. They used the area's underground river system as their own private hunting grounds and migratory system all rolled into one. Nasty things, mermaids.

Standing on the lip of this gateway into the Halls, I kept flashing back to those weeks spent at Blue Hole. How often had I swam there as bait, expecting a hand to grab my ankle and drag me to a watery grave, trusting Shaw's reflexes were fast enough to save me if something tried?

I hoped we washed ashore after confronting what awaited us in the deep.

"It's an illusion," Rook said under his breath. "You have nothing to fear."

The Watchers each stepped to one side of the hole and waited. I guess we were going first.

The soothing presence at my side had vanished. I sought out Diode. "Are you coming?"

"If I must." He pressed against me and scowled at his reflection in the water. "Disgusting."

"You'll be fine." I clutched his ruff. "If you're not, you can take it out of Rook's hide."

"Pleased to be of service," Rook said dryly.

I patted his chest. "I never doubted."

"The consuls await," the Watchers reminded us.

I tried meeting their eye—eyes?—and ended up crossing mine. "Can't have that, can we?"

Rook cleared his throat. "Everything you say and do before them is seen by the consuls."

"I figured." I stood on the edge of the pool. "I just don't care."

They had kept me bent over a barrel since I arrived, hell, before I arrived, and I just wanted to go home. I had participated. That meant Mom went free. The rest wasn't outlined, and I hadn't signed any papers. Our verbal agreement, my obligation, was met to the letter.

Rook slid his hand into mine. I squeezed his fingers and let him guide me. We stepped onto, not into, the water. The sensation of falling tensed my knees, but he kept me standing as the water rose, never touching us, and the pit of my stomach stopped hovering overhead and dropped back into place.

Once the illusion of water receded, we stood in a cylindrical room made of what must have been glass or crystal. Beneath us, water rushed. It cascaded down the sides too. Overhead, a circular patch of blue sky illuminated the uncluttered chamber.

A low growl pumped to my left. Diode's fur bristled, making him twice as imposing.

Poor guy, this had to be a cat's worst nightmare.

A breeze stirred the loose hairs hanging from my braid, announcing the Watchers had joined us in the chamber. They crossed the room to where two clear benches extended from the wall, and sat. Over their heads, the rushing waters parted, and the same two likenesses as before appeared as watercolor portraits. Neither of the consuls looked pleased to see me.

"Thierry Thackeray." Liosliath inspected me. "Your presence here is…most unexpected."

"You agreed to take your father's place in exchange for the return of your mother." Daibhidh stared daggers at me. "Yet there you stand, as he has never stood."

"Sorry, guys." I kept my tone neutral. "This Black Dog gig didn't come with an instruction manual."

Air distorted to my right, and the Huntsman appeared with a snort.

"You laugh at this?" Liosliath spoke. "She murdered your hounds in cold blood."

"Cold?" He chuckled. "No. Cold-blooded would be stealing a girl's mother, ripping her from her life to participate in a game you savor playing every century. That this is the first time one of your houses has broken their blood oath and murdered a reigning king is the only surprise here."

Liosliath's reflection rippled with the force of his anger.

"This is not the first time a prince has died in pursuit of the throne, nor will it be the last. How many times have we crowned kings while their rival's blood still stained their teeth?" The Huntsman drew himself taller. "The loss of both princes in one hunt is regrettable, but as we have offered past victors amnesty for crimes they committed in the heat of battle, so must we make allowances now."

"Do the lives in your care mean so little?" Daibhidh asked.

"My hounds die in this tourney. Just as princes do. The beasts are made from my own blood and bone, my own soul and thought. When they die, it is *I* who pays the price," he snarled. "Never think I don't mourn their loss."

The anguish in his voice resonated with me. "I'm sorry for my part in their deaths."

"No one is truly sorry when they won and lived." He sighed. "But I do accept the sentiment."

"We sit here discussing *dogs* when each of the houses has lost a *prince*." Daibhidh glared.

"The question set before us is this—" Liosliath spread his hands, "—do we forgive your trespass, allow you to atone by offering yourself as tribute for the next hunt, or do we behead you now as recompense?"

Rook stepped forward. "I propose a third alternative."

That same taste of apprehension soured my mouth.

The Huntsman cocked his head. "What do you propose?"

"Your final words were, I believe, 'May the best hound win.'" Rook addressed Liosliath's image with a tight smile then swept out his arm to indicate me. "I would argue that the best hound did."

Utter silence. Complete stillness.

Then the room caught its breath and the consuls exploded into shouted arguments with Rook.

"Silence," the Huntsman bellowed. "I will have silence."

"The fact remains." Liosliath cleared his throat. "She is not a hound."

"She is the daughter of Black Dog, who once led the Wild Hunt and was one of the Huntsman's first and best hounds." Rook snapped his fingers, and the Unseelie prince's pelt appeared draped across my shoulders. "She claimed my brother's skin as hers. She was a hound when she slayed the Seelie prince."

"You are no doubt claiming this was an Unseelie victory," Liosliath seethed.

Daibhidh's reflection jolted as he grasped the implications.

"Perhaps we ought to hear him out," he said thoughtfully.

"You can't be serious," Liosliath spluttered. "She killed our princes."

Daibhidh waved a hand. "There are more princes where those came from." He swept his gaze over me with renewed interest. "Now a princess...that would be unique."

My jaw would have dropped if I hadn't clenched it shut.

"A princess," Liosliath echoed with a grimace.

"An *Unseelie* princess," his counterpart confirmed.

"If we allowed her to ascend," Liosliath argued, "she must replace the king *we* lost. She must become a Seelie princess if such a title is bestowed, and how can it be? She is neutral, if you recall."

Again Rook cleared his throat. "What small knowledge I have gleaned from her and her father's condition leads me to assume that she devoured Raven's essence prior to his death and the removal of his skin. That means my brother was with Thierry, physically and spiritually, as the Seelie prince died."

"If she becomes a crown princess," Liosliath argued, "what of her position in her world?"

My job, my life, my income was all being decided right in front of me like I wasn't even there.

"I don't want a crown," I spoke over them. "I don't want to rule."

I had come to love my position with the conclave. I would not be blackmailed into this.

Rook returned to my side and gathered my hands in his. His thumbs rolled across my knuckles. "You won't have to," he promised me in a low tone. He then projected his voice for the High Court's benefit. "My wife is young and modern. She was raised among humans. Thierry doesn't understand the ways and traditions of Faerie, as evidenced by the fact we are all standing here having this conversation."

"Don't sound so disappointed not to be rid of her," the Huntsman rumbled.

"You can't comprehend the depths of my gratitude that she survived the ordeal." He touched my cheek. "A lesser woman would have fallen victim to the hounds. Mine tore the skin from those who dared hunt her and ended their lives for their trespass against her. She is worthy of any crown."

"As I recall…" Liosliath folded his arms, "…she is not alone in her humble origins. It seems to me that you were one of the Morrigan's follies among men. Only she chose to raise you alongside her heir after her lord husband learned of your existence and threatened to see her wings clipped permanently. Your origin is as clouded as your bride's, Rook Morriganson."

"I lived twelve years among men," Rook answered. "I have lived centuries among the sidhe."

Face lit with avarice, Daibhidh asked, "What are you proposing?"

"That I rule in her stead," he said in a loud, clear voice so steady he must have practiced the line.

My head whipped toward him so fast I got a crick in my neck. From pauper to princess—or was it from fae queen to Rook's pawn?—in under five minutes. That must break a Faerie dynastic record.

Beware the Rook. I was growing warier by the minute.

Diode snarled under his breath.

"Ha." The Huntsman tugged at his beard. "What have you done to earn the right to rule?"

"More than my brother ever did." Rook aimed his next remarks toward the consuls. "My crime was the circumstance of my birth, over which I had no control. I have been a loyalist of House Unseelie. I have sweated and bled and toiled—" his gaze touched on mine, "—and I have lied for them."

"Be that as it may, you can't believe even your own people will obey you." Liosliath frowned. "If you seek to sell us on Thierry's merits—you have done so. She is worthy of her father's legacy, but it does you and yours no good to thrust the girl upon a throne she does not want and will not occupy."

"She is fatigued from her ordeal," Daibhidh countered. "Once she has recovered, she will see this unprecedented opportunity for the gift it is. Let her head clear before she answers."

"She is half mortal," the Huntsman contributed. "She has eaten and slept little since the hunt began."

"A recession might be the best thing for it." Liosliath sighed. "We will not reach an agreement lightly or swiftly. We have heard all the testimony from the tribute and her husband we require." He glanced at the Watcher below him. "The final sequence of events we must view with our own eyes."

As one, the Watchers stood and crossed to the wall opposite the consul's images.

"Bring food and wine for them both." The Huntsman's lips curved. "Prepare them a room."

Heat stung my cheeks. Let them think they had made me blush. Anger burns brighter red, I think.

Share a room with Rook.

I would be delighted.

CHAPTER TWENTY-EIGHT

An autumnal dryad escorted us to our room. I knew her by the vines tying back her yellow-orange hair and the rust-colored leaves tucked into her braids. Her skin was light brown and the tops of her arms rough like pine bark.

Under different circumstances, I might have been awed by our accommodations, the way rays of sunlight warmed my skin through the sky-lit ceiling or how the tranquil blue wallpaper offered an illusion of privacy. Driftwood furniture bleached white by the sun called to mind long hot summers spent on Galveston Island. Periwinkle and sage accents reminded me of home, of the bungalow where I grew up, not the cookie-cutter subdivision where the conclave stashed Mom and me so they could keep an eye on us.

"The High Court will reconvene tomorrow morning." Her voice rustled like leaves stirred by gentle winds. "Until such time, I ask that you remain here in the quarters provided for you." She reached in her hair and removed an ornament—a garden snail's circular shell—and offered it to me. I accepted, and it grew to fill my palm. "Speak into the spout if you have need of me. I will hear your command and obey. The steward will be around soon with food, wine and changes of clothes for each of you."

I patted Diode's shoulders. "My friend is also tired and hungry."

The dryad's lips pursed. "I will see that a meal and bedding to his liking will also be provided."

"Tha—" I clamped my mouth shut. "I appreciate your efforts on our behalf."

She dropped into a curtsy made elegant by the simple earth-toned dress she wore.

When she left, she shut the door behind her. I locked it and braced my forehead against it.

Rook eased behind me, and the weight of his brother's pelt vanished. He slid his arms around my waist and rested his chin on my shoulder.

Facing the carved panels was easier than looking at him. "Did you kill King Moran?"

"No."

I nodded, not sure I believed him. "Did you kidnap my mother?"

A slight pause. "No."

My throat tightened. "Was it your idea?"

A longer pause. "Yes."

Slowly, I pushed away from the door. Rook stepped back and gave me room to face him. I rested my hands on his shoulders and studied his fathomless eyes for a scrap of remorse. Finding none, I used my grip as leverage, brought my knee up hard to his groin and ruined his chances of siring any heirs. I waited for a wheeze of pure masculine pain then shoved him aside and stalked across the room to Diode.

"Your mother..." Rook cleared his throat and gingerly straightened his shoulders, "...is safe."

I tucked my hands under my arms to prevent myself from wringing his neck. "How safe?"

"She's at my home." His chest heaved. "Bháin is protecting her."

So close. I had been so near her and had no clue. All of this, the hunt, the deaths, for nothing.

"She was there." I took a step. "My mom was in your house, and you didn't tell me? I could have taken her home. None of this had to happen. People *died*." I took another step. "I killed for you. None of this was for her. None of this was about me or Macsen. This whole thing was about you."

"I had no choice."

"Did my father really fall off the radar, or did you offer him the guest suite across from Mom's?"

"Your father is, as far as anyone knows, still tracking King Moran's killer. The parts of Faerie you have seen are tame. I kept you to the safe roads, the light places. Much of Faerie grows wild. He is a hunter. He won't rest until he finds his mark."

"Diode?" I glanced at the unusually quiet cat. "Is that true?"

The cat's broad jaw flexed. All of this was Macsen's current business. That explained Diode's silence.

I sank into one of the chairs near an end table. I couldn't look at Rook. "Tell me you didn't set all this into motion."

"Rooks are opportunistic pests." Diode found his voice and hissed. "Filthy scavengers."

"He's right," Rook admitted. "When King Moran's death was announced, it marked the end of an era. Since your father's appointment, there have been no assassinations. The truce between courts has been upheld because your father led the High Court, and he, along with the consuls, mediated before disputes ended in bloodshed. But now all that will change. Already there are those eager to use Moran's death as cause for war." He dragged a hand through his hair. "Peace doesn't come naturally to the sidhe. It has been imposed upon us by those laid low by war. Amnesty worked far better than anyone expected but—"

I leaned back and crossed my feet at the ankles. "I knew a *but* was coming."

"—but if war is coming," he continued, "then I want my people to be on the right side of it."

The right side of war was an illusion. You couldn't *win* a war. There was too much loss.

"Is it that big a deal that the Unseelie haven't ruled in…?" Now that I thought about it, I couldn't think of a time when they had held the upper hand in Faerie. "I'm asking you—does it matter so much?"

"The Unseelie are but a means to an end." He stepped toward me, heard Diode snarl and turned. "What matters to me isn't my house, but my people—the other half-bloods trapped in servitude here. Not everyone is like us, Thierry. Not all fae born have even one loving parent or a safe place to rest."

"All this because you want to liberate the half-bloods?" I heard the doubt in my voice.

"I want them exiled from Faerie and sent to the mortal realm where they have a chance at a good life."

Part of me, the old me, the one who had thought she was human, whose mother kissed every boo-boo and bought cookies from our favorite bakery on special occasions, wished all children—human, fae or other—had that kind of champion in their lives. The other part, the one honed by a conclave education, staggered under the realization of what a mass exodus from Faerie meant for humans. People would die. Lots of them.

Kids just like I had been would find themselves in the mortal realm and make the same mistakes as me. One or two kids would throw the conclave a curve ball. What Rook proposed numbered in the hundreds, and he said it was for all half-bloods. Children were the most unpredictable, but teens were volatile. Depending on the intensity of their gifts and their ability to control those powers, some adults weren't much better.

Rook was talking about dumping sharks into a goldfish bowl. "I don't think exile is the answer."

"Exile means even the missing among the half-bloods must be accounted for and returned."

I furrowed my brow. "Missing?"

"You are Black Dog's only known child. That makes you unique." A cruel twist of his lips. "As the Morrigan's bastard, I am much more common."

The anxious twitch in my foot stopped. "What are you saying?"

A whiff of subtle magic tickled my nose.

Rook straightened his shoulders, jutted out his chin and dared me to look away from the force of his unrelenting attention. "I have a sister." I saw his lips move more than heard the words. He was in my face, his hand clasped gently around my throat, his thumb caressing my fluttering pulse, before I could blink, before even Diode registered his intent. "Never speak of her again. Do you understand?"

That explained the scent. He had cast a privacy enchantment on the room.

"It depends..." I leaned forward, pressing my throat hard against his palm, "...on how well you understand me. Touch my mother again, mention her in conversation or even breathe the same air as she does without my permission, and I'll hit up Quick Copy and print out flyers with every ounce of information the conclave has on your sister. Then I'll hitch a ride here and plaster Faerie with them."

"Don't make me kill you." He sounded more tired than threatening.

"Oh, I don't know." My grin showed teeth. "If your princess kicks the bucket, then I'm guessing that means you lose your position too. That puts you right back where you started from, and—as you pointed out—my father only made one mistake. Kill me, and it's game over."

He released me. "You realize if they don't make you princess, they will kill you."

"I figured."

Scowling all the while, Rook withdrew and began pacing.

When that started annoying me, I blurted out the question making my heart burn. "If they decide in my favor, what happens to me? I meant what I said. I don't want a crown or a title or a throne." It was on the tip of my tongue to add I didn't want a husband either, but our union, as much as it grated on me, might be the only thing keeping me alive. "No one will believe I'm neutral if I'm tangled up in all of this."

"Has it never occurred to you that you aren't meant to be neutral?" he mused. "The very nature of your gift, even your origin, is all rooted in the Unseelie house."

The notion I could or should pick a side had honestly never occurred to me. Since that very first day in Mable's office, I had heard my father's praises sung and had the mantle of his legacy settled around my shoulders.

Rook must have realized the direction of my thoughts and paused. "Has it never dawned on you the reason the conclave filled your head with stories of your father wasn't because they believed you were meant to spread his tenets, but because it was safer for them if you believed that was the case?"

"They gave me a choice—join or die." I frowned. "What does belief have to do with it?"

"You were more powerful than any of them expected. Either side would fight a war to have you join their cause if the truce is broken." He spread his hands. "Control over the infamous Black Dog's legendary powers, unfettered by his morals, free of the compulsion that is the fabric of his identity."

"There's one small problem with your theory," I interrupted. "I'm not all that powerful."

Black Dog might be my father, but the fraction I inherited wasn't the sum of his whole.

Rook cast me a pitying glance, one that made the foundation of my life quake yet again. "Did all the half-bloods employed by the conclave receive the same join-or-die memo from the magistrates you did?"

"No." I shifted in my seat. "But not all of them killed five humans in one whack, either."

"Think about your situation like this. Your father is unique among the fae. You, as his daughter, share his rare qualities. You are comparing your powers to his, which are vast and uncharted. That is your mistake," he said. "Your gifts should be measured against the known limits of half-blood magic."

I glanced to Diode for confirmation. "Is he spouting crazy, or is it just me?"

"I can say this—" he struggled to move his lips, "—most fae children are given a choice, and they aren't issued conclave guardians."

I didn't like the sound of that. It made me reevaluate every interaction I had ever had with Mable, and with Shaw. "They wanted me to have a protector."

The big cat jerked his head. "Not you. Everyone else."

Rising from my chair, I walked to the bed and climbed onto the mattress.

Rook frowned at me. "Is now the best time for a nap?"

"I have to go to sleep." My head hit the pillow. "How else can I wake up from this nightmare?"

CHAPTER TWENTY-NINE

The guys let me sleep through dinner. When I woke, the room was bathed in moonlight and they had staked out opposing corners. Sleeping. Diode sprawled over a velvet comforter while Rook dozed slouched in a plush chair by the door. I sat upright and hung my feet over the edge of the bed. My weary exhale brought Rook's eyes open a slit. Once he saw I was awake, he stifled a yawn.

After stretching, he crossed the room to a small table where a seashell-encrusted tray sat beside a blue milk glass pitcher with matching cups. "They brought fresh fruit. All Earth varieties." White mist curled under the lid when he lifted it. "Watermelon, cantaloupe, grapes and blackberries. Are you hungry?"

"Not really." I untied my hair and combed my fingers through the worst knots.

"You should eat." Diode didn't twitch a paw. "You need your strength."

Rook nudged my shoulder with the edge of a plate. "He's right. You have to eat something."

I folded my legs under me, picked up a strawberry and brought it to my lips. Rook watched with rapt attention, and I don't think I was the only one remembering how I had fed him berries in the burrow. The act had been impersonal then. There was nothing indifferent about the way he watched me now.

Too bad I wasn't in the mood. I stopped eating until he took the hint and returned to his chair.

Passing over the berry, I chose a cube of watermelon. "How much longer do you think?"

"An hour, maybe less." He stretched his legs out in front of him and crossed his ankles. He must have noticed my eyebrows creeping upward. He qualified, "The dryad has been keeping us updated."

I rolled my eyes and bit into another piece of fruit. "I bet she has."

His lips quirked in a pleased kind of almost smile that would have done flip-floppy things to my stomach yesterday. Today I was reconciled to my fate.

Fine. So I liked him. No. I *had* liked him before grasping the depth of his betrayal.

The time was right wasn't an excuse. For the greater good, well, that wasn't much of one either. Not unless I had concrete evidence another party benefitted from his scheming. Right now I had nothing. Just his word, a spark of believable anger and the hope he had told me the truth.

For once.

I didn't want Rook to have a missing sibling, but knowledge was power. If she existed, and if he had orchestrated all of this to find her, then I had twenty-four-karat leverage.

Soft knocks on the door had me setting aside my plate and sliding from the mattress to my feet.

"Come in," Rook called after joining me.

The dryad entered with a smile that wilted as her gaze swept over me. "You have not changed."

I cast Rook a *what is that about* look.

"The garments you provided for Thierry are lovely, but I noticed the buttons bear the crest of the Seelie house." His lips thinned. "The consuls will understand why she must decline to wear items that might mistakenly imply her loyalty to an opposing faction. She is wed to an Unseelie."

Red splashed over her cheeks. "I am sure the consuls meant no disrespect."

Since she looked to me, I forced a smile. "I'm sure it was an innocent mistake."

Ah, politics. As far as anyone knew, my head was as likely to be severed as it was to be crowned. The Seelie were hedging their bets. But buttons? Really? Then again, if broth and a change of clothes had made me Rook's common-law wife, who knew what a button signified?

I was starting to think the dead princes were the lucky ones. Who would choose this kind of life?

Rook touched my arm, jarring me from my thoughts and answering that question. He wanted it. He had chosen this life, possibly for both of us. Had schemed and wheedled and toiled to possess it.

"The consuls await your arrival." She kept her head bowed. "I will escort you if you are ready."

"I'm ready." I rolled my shoulders, loosening them. "Diode?"

The grumpy cat rose and stretched, yawning in a way that showcased all of his sizable teeth. He padded over to me and headbutted my thigh to get me moving. "Go on, you will not face this alone."

My fingers curled in his fur. Rook came to my side but made no move to touch me. Smart man.

After nudging Rook out the door ahead of us, I paused while he and the dryad got a head start. I knelt in front of Diode, putting us eye to eye. "If this goes south, I need you to promise me something."

He rubbed his soft cheek against mine. "Of course."

"Make sure Mom gets home." I swallowed. "She won't want details. Just—let her make up her own mind about what happened to me. If you hung around for a while…after…that would be good too."

His tongue rasped against the tip of my nose. "She will want for nothing, and no harm will come to her so long as I live."

I wiped the backs of my hands under my eyes. "You're not half bad for a cat."

"If I had found you as a pup," he said on a chuckle, "I might not have drowned you either."

Haggard faces greeted us inside the chamber. The Watchers, the Huntsman and the consuls waited exactly where we had left them.

"The consuls have come to an agreement," Liosliath announced.

"Will you agree to abide by our ruling?" Daibhidh's voice crackled with glee. "Well?"

I exchanged a glance with Diode and then with Rook. Each offered me a nod of encouragement. "I…" I balled my fists until my nails cut crescent moons in my palms. "I will accept your judgment."

The Huntsman grunted at the consuls then approached me. Rook eased between us, but I shoved him aside and faced my judgment alone. My Word rested on my lips, ready to leap from my tongue. I may have exaggerated a skosh about the acceptance thing. I had come too far to meekly accept death.

The consuls would have a fight on their hands if they wanted to put down this little black dog.

The Huntsman held out his hands, curling his fingers until I placed mine in his.

"Thierry Thackeray, daughter of Macsen Sullivan, it is with a glad heart I welcome you to Faerie." He brought my hands to his mouth and kissed my knuckles. "I wish your sire might see you now. He would be as proud of you as I am, for we are kin, as your father was knit together from my flesh and bones and so you were from his. You may call on me in times of need. I am loyal to your reign."

My lips parted, but all I managed was to bob my head in response.

"Long live Princess Thierry," he bellowed, "champion of House Unseelie, beloved daughter of the Black Dog, wife of the Rook, daughter-in-law of the Morrigan, granddaughter of my heart…"

Struck mute by his recitation, it hit me what he was doing. Here, before these witnesses, he was claiming me. He was warning both courts who my allies were so they knew who they would answer to if I was harmed. The message was clear. Their prince had been murdered, their princess wouldn't be.

Quick as a rabbit, my heart jumped around in my chest. *They're going to let me live.*

Daibhidh's reflection beamed at me while a somber Liosliath kept his own council.

Swaying on my feet, I let the Huntsman's meaty hand clasp my shoulder and hold me steady.

"We will relinquish the crown in seven days," Liosliath granted.

"We will remove Prince Raven's belongings from the Halls of Winter." Daibhidh grinned. "It is now your home to do with as you see fit." He addressed Rook. "No doubt your husband can help smooth your transition to court life. I offer my council to you, Princess, whenever you are in need. I am your humble servant."

Home. Home was a realm away. My family, my friends, my life—none of it was here.

Rook must have sensed me teetering on the breaking point. He wrapped an arm around me, and I let him support me because my knees had turned to water. His soft lips brushed the shell of my ear.

"Relax," he whispered. "The worst is over."

No. My life was over.

His clear voice pierced through the excited murmurings. "The princess does have one request."

Liosliath's brow puckered. "We are listening."

"As overcome as she is by her great fortune, she desires a period of five years during which time she will transition from life in the mortal realm to life here. She wishes to familiarize herself with the intricacies of her new position before she assumes official duties." He squeezed me tighter against him. "Five years is a blink of time."

The consuls' likenesses darkened, and their respective Watchers shifted on their seats.

"We offer you a crown, and you refuse it in favor of living among—among *humans*?" Hot color boiled in Daibhidh's cheeks. "You seek to make a mockery of the mercy we have shown you."

The Huntsman growled at them. "You would rescue her from the hounds and throw her to the wolves?"

"I rescued myself." The words popped out before I thought to stop them.

"What do you mean?" Liosliath asked the Huntsman, "What are you implying?"

"She was raised as a human by a human." The Huntsman spread his hands. Point made. "The Southwestern Conclave provided her with a basic education on fae politics as they exist in the mortal realm. Allow her twelve months, a mere year of her centennial reign, as preparation to assume the throne."

The reflections rippled in contemplation.

"Who do you propose rules during that time?" Liosliath asked at last.

The Huntsman worked his jaw, chewing over his answer for a full minute before he sighed. "I propose Rook be named our Prince Regent and given the power to act on the princess's behalf during her absence."

"Absence?" Liosliath and Daibhidh's voices echoed.

The Huntsman lifted his hand. "I propose she be allowed to continue her education in the mortal realm." When Liosliath started to argue, Huntsman said, "After her coronation, she will be bound to our realm and expected to leave her old life behind her. She is young, with living mortal relatives. There is also the matter of justice for King Moran. While his killer remains free, we remain ignorant of his reasons for assassinating the king. Until he is punished, the princess may also be in danger."

"Are you implying that the Conclave and its marshals are more capable of safeguarding our princess than we are?" Daibhidh sneered. "Her infamy is what will protect her. Don't be a fool."

"I think his idea has merit." Liosliath's expression turned thoughtful. "I second the idea."

"*What?*" his counterpart screeched.

While those two hurled insults at one another, the Huntsman edged closer to me and interpreted.

"Consul Liosliath must believe if you're in the mortal realm that those laws will apply when he tries to have you killed. Some might argue that since you were mortal born, they apply regardless."

The Seelie consul excelled at reading people. He knew if he let me go home, I would fight tooth and claw to stay there. And I would. The law the Huntsman spoke of stated if you left Faerie, permanently, as I wanted to, you severed all ties with your family. Therefore, if the Seelie had me killed, no one of my bloodline in Faerie could seek vengeance.

"That's a clever interpretation of the law," I allowed. "Why is Daibhidh pissed?"

"You're the first princess of any house. You would be the first Unseelie to rule since your father's writ became law. Not only that. News of your win will spread like wild faefire through both realms." He grunted. "Consul Daibhidh wants to ensure your reign sticks, and the best way to do that is to put you on display, to spread stories of your victories and leak the footage gathered by the Watchers. There is also the matter of your vows to Rook. While he is not a catch by anyone's standards, he is Unseelie."

Defense for Rook pursed my lips. Then I thought of my mom, and the urge vanished. "Care to tell me what the real reason is why I'm getting even a temporary *get out of jail free* ticket?"

His chuckle rumbled under his breath. "Fae are star born and sun forged. This notion of peaceful living was a new idea to old minds. Old ones prize novelty as much as they fear the change it brings. It is never a certainty whether curiosity or self-preservation will triumph. We all thought 'What harm can come of living this way?' Longevity, stability and wealth were the benefits Black Dog extoled."

"Faerie thrived under those laws." Or so the conclave assured us.

"Aye, she did, for a while. Now those laws are poison ink seeping beneath her parchment skin."

I frowned. "What do you mean?"

"The truce was signed with blood, locking us into a forced peace, which causes dissent to ripple beneath the surface of every conversation. This is not a natural state of being. This is not as it should be. Peace is an empty gesture when it must be maintained by force. Your father has exhausted himself for his beliefs, and I admire his dedication, but the old truce was broken when King Moran died."

"If the truce is broken and everyone wants out," I wondered, "why bother with any of this?"

"It's sleight of hand, child. Smoke and mirrors. Present your enemies the face you wish them to see while concealing your true intentions. You are a final hope for your father's writ. The people will either follow you out of loyalty for him and respect for how you obtained the crown, or they will rebel and blood will fall like rain across the land." He exhaled. "Truth be told, it would almost be a relief."

With a mighty sigh, the Huntsman strode toward the Watchers and addressed the consuls.

Diode issued a deep purr, drawing my attention down to him. I got the message. We weren't leaving any time soon, so I ought to put my hands to good use.

From the corner of my eye, I noticed Rook. He stood with his shoulders back and his face wiped of emotion. His eyes, though, burned bright. Anticipation rolled off him until my nerves jittered. Pride. That was what I saw in him. Ambition too. Beneath the obvious I saw the boy he had once described, who must have ached to belong to this backstabbing fae world. He wet his lips, no doubt tasting his elusive acceptance.

Deep wounds only festered if they were left untreated. Rook's could use a smear of Neosporin.

Looking at him, I hoped I wasn't staring into my future. I had daddy issues. Hell, I had mommy issues too. Who didn't? But I had to believe I could let go of my anger where the first was concerned and smooth bumps in the second before it was too late. Rook wasn't looking to heal. Maybe if I...

No. Rook was not my problem. Smile and wave, grab Mom then burn rubber getting home. That was the plan. No pit stops in Redemptionville. You had to want to be saved. No one could want it for you. Change wouldn't stick if you built Teflon walls around yourself. Nope. Fixing him was his job.

"Princess."

I continued chewing my bottom lip.

"Princess?"

Claws pierced the meat of my thigh. I bit down hard to stop the scream trapped in my throat and glared at Diode, who cut his eyes toward the waiting consuls.

Oh. Yeah. *Princess.*

That would be me.

I corrected my slouch and tried sounding solemn. "Yes?"

"The case made on your behalf has its merits," Liosliath allowed. "You may be in grave danger. We have granted others temporary pardons from their duties under similar circumstances. Also, we feel that in light of your upbringing, formal training would not go amiss before you ascend to the throne. Your husband can see to that.

"We have decided to grant you one year to prepare yourself for your new position. We will set your coronation date one year from today. During that time, your husband will rule in your stead as Prince Regent of Faerie."

"Do you find those terms agreeable?" Daibhidh asked with grim resolve.

"I do." Freedom loomed so close I could taste tomorrow's breakfast burrito.

"Then we are all in agreement," the Huntsman boomed.

"I do have one last question." I kept my voice level. "When will my mother be returned to me?"

The consuls shrugged in unison.

"That is a civil matter," Liosliath said. Daibhidh agreed. "Your husband has those details."

The tiny drop of pity I had felt for Rook evaporated. A civil matter, they said. Ask my husband, they said. They didn't care. Not about Mom's health or her wellbeing or her happiness. She was a human whose life mattered less to them than the pixies my father kept jarred.

How could I learn to care for this realm or its politics when neither cared anything for me?

CHAPTER THIRTY

My knees lasted a dozen steps away from the Halls of Summer's watery portal before collapsing. One minute I was walking with my fingers clutching Diode's ruff, the next I hit the ground.

Rook tugged me to my feet and slung his arm around my waist. "It's over."

"No." I resented how I leaned against him. "It's just beginning."

As much as I wanted to pull away, I wanted to escape from the consuls and their Watchers more. I let him help me into the relative safety of Spring before slipping from his grasp and walking alone.

Diode padded beside me, his thick brow furrowed and his long tail marking time behind him.

No one spoke. Preserving our tentative peace meant keeping our mouths shut.

A trick of time sped our crossing through Spring. Maybe I was too lost in my thoughts to notice until the slap of frigid winds across my cheeks stung me into alertness. We had arrived in Winter. Suddenly, I was glad I hadn't changed from my protective clothes.

Rook's icy home was invisible amid the whirling snowflakes until I stumbled over a path leading to its door. The calmness that had insulated me for the past several hours shattered as my fist hit the wood.

Rook caught my wrist. "Stop before you break your hand."

"Open it," I snarled.

"I can't." He glanced overhead. "The premises are enchanted. I keyed the spell to Bháin before I left. He knows we're here. Be patient. Give him time to reach the door before you break it down."

Diode bumped his broad head against my hip. Even in his silence, he was siding with Rook.

Not one minute passed, not two or three. Not even four, but five whole minutes ticked past, counted out by my tapping foot, before Bháin greeted us. Dismissing Rook with a bland smirk, he bowed. To me.

"Princess Thierry." His voice shivered down my spine. "It is gratifying to see you again."

I peered up at him. "How did you...?"

"I hear things." He lifted his hand, and a snowflake danced across his palm. "Word travels fast."

"What can I say?" I edged past him into the house. "I'm harder to kill than I look."

He stepped aside as Rook entered, and didn't blink at Diode. "Can I prepare—?"

"Cut the crap." I pinched the bridge of my nose. "Take me to my mother."

He exchanged a calm glance with Rook.

I stepped between them, though they could see over my head. I snapped my fingers in Bháin's face. "Now."

With a formal bow that dripped sarcasm, Bháin turned on his heel. "Follow me."

He guided me past the fireplace where the elemental leapt to its feet, glowing in cheery welcome. Unfamiliar with elemental courtesies, I smiled on my way past. Bháin sauntered down the winding hall to the right of the foyer. More portraits of death and dismemberment hung on the walls. I wondered what Mom had thought of them. Had she walked these halls? Been carried? Blindfolded?

Try as I might, I couldn't dredge up the courage to ask.

"Here we are." He knocked twice. "Agnes?"

"Come in. I'm decent." With a husky chuckle, she added, "For now."

Bháin found anywhere other than at me to look. "You have a visitor."

"Oh, really?" She tittered. "Giovani, I'm no spring chicken. I can't keep up with—"

I shoved him aside and opened the door before I tossed my cookies. *"Mom."*

There she was, reclining on a lounger with a magazine on her lap and a sunhat on her head. She wore the same yellow and black rose swimsuit, except the top had come undone and the ties were wound around her fingers. *Ew. Ew. Ew.* I blinked a few times, testing if I had been blinded for life by her nip slip.

Mom was perfectly safe, perfectly sound, and scarring me for life with her pool-boy shenanigans.

"Thierry?" She flattened the magazine against her chest. "What on earth are you doing here?"

"I could ask you the same thing."

My first step into the room confused the hell out of me.

Gone were the ice-block walls. There were no walls period. I had stepped from ice floors onto the powdery sands of Galveston Island. Blues skies stretched into forever. Waves crashed as gulls cried. I trudged through the sand to her lounger, plopped down and just breathed the briny air for a minute.

"I told you I was going to visit Marcia and Stan for the weekend." She leaned forward and retied her top. "They're at the bar getting us drinks. You look flushed. Do you need a bottled water?"

"No." I scooted closer and rested my head against her side. "I'm fine."

She pushed the hairs from my eyes and pressed the back of her hand to my forehead. "You don't feel hot." She checked the sides of my throat for swelling. "Is your throat sore? Have you been coughing?"

I took her hands in mine. "I'm good, really."

She sighed. "You never said why you're here."

It stung how eager she was to shoo me off and get back to flirting with men who looked half her age but were probably older than the sand under my butt. By all appearances, she was having a blast. She hadn't even noticed my getup. Maybe that was part of the illusion too.

I glanced over my shoulder and saw the freestanding door a few dunes away from us.

All of this was one complex visual and audial illusion. This beach, that particular couple—who I knew Mom hadn't spoken to since I killed their daughter Andrea—all the details were pulled straight from her memory. Bháin was powerful if he could create such a vivid false reality and maintain it for days on end. Fondness for him oozed from her voice. He had played along to make her comfortable. Just how comfortable I *never* wanted to find out.

I didn't know what to make of this, of any of this. I had pictured her lost and alone and terrified. I envisioned her in the same situation as me. Fear for her had motivated me. Now I felt so...deflated. I almost relished pulling her from this fantasy back to cold reality.

"I got a call from Andy." I swallowed the lump in my throat. Using Andrea's nickname hurt. "She needs her room—"

"Did something happen at Baylor?" She sat upright. "Is she all right?"

No, Mom. She's not. She's never going to be all right again. "She's fine."

"Oh. Well." Mom settled back into a relaxed position. "I have been here a few days. I can cut my trip short if she's coming home for a visit." A sharp frown cut across her face. "I haven't seen Andrea in a long time. Years it feels like. Her poor parents. Andy's class schedule must keep her busy."

Baylor. Class schedule. Apparently, not all of this was pure memory. Andrea hadn't survived to college age. Part of this illusion was threaded with Mom's dreams for us and plans Andy and I had made together.

Suddenly, I had to find somewhere else to look. That's when Rook caught my eye. He stood in the doorway, framed like a chilly memory of winter in summer's heart. He noticed me watching and stepped out of sight.

How much of this was his doing? How much of the care shown to her was at his request? Bháin had argued with him before we left. Over this? Over her? Which one did I have to thank for keeping her blissfully unaware of her circumstances? Who was my heart softening toward? Rook? Or Bháin?

"Do you mind if I finish my drink first?"

Mom's voice drew my attention back to her. "No. Go ahead. I'll go hit the bathroom before we leave."

While she settled in to wait for a drink I wasn't sure would come, I crossed the shifting sand and stepped back into the hall. The sudden dimness after the full sunlight made me stagger. Strong hands grasped my upper arms until my eyes adjusted, guiding me until my back hit the wall and I steadied.

Rook loomed over me. I waited for the urge to rip him a new one, but it never showed.

I exhaled through my teeth. "We need to talk about how long this mind warp is going to last."

His hands slid down to my wrists, fingers brushing fingers. "Forever unless you say otherwise."

"The memories you pulled—" I began.

He shook his head. "That was Bháin's doing."

"Okay, the memories Bháin pulled aren't good ones." At his puzzled expression, I added, "She's in there, thinking she's on the beach where we used to live, waiting to drink with friends she doesn't have anymore because I killed their daughter. When she snaps out of it, she'll know it wasn't real."

"What do you want me to do?"

Mom deserved to know the truth. She deserved to know what had happened to us both. She was here because of me, and it was wrong for me to make this decision for her, but I had to make the call. I had to be strong enough for both of us.

"She goes on singles cruises sometimes." I rubbed my forehead. "She would believe that. They board in Galveston. I think that's half the reason she takes them, just to have an excuse to fly down."

"Explain the concept to Bháin, and he will do the rest."

I shifted so I could keep an eye on Mom. "How are we getting home?"

"I will escort you through the tether." His voice softened. "Then I must return."

"You got everything you wanted." An edge of fresh anger crept into my tone.

His gaze held mine. "Not everything."

"Word is spreading quickly," Bháin reminded us. "If Thierry wants to cross realms unmolested, she must leave soon." He leaned against the door, watching my mother while he spoke to me. "There will be those who seek to do you harm, those who you counted as friends before you chose a side."

"I haven't picked a side." I scowled at him. "I'm the freaking interim Black Dog."

"The Black Dog is impartial. It was understood you relinquished that title when you accepted your new appointment." He glanced my way. "Whether you like it or not, you're the Unseelie princess now."

I set my jaw. Better to keep quiet than provoke him into lobotomizing my mom.

"You can take a vow of neutrality," Rook said. "You can keep your position with the conclave, for now."

"Those vows don't come with an expiration date." Once spoken, they were binding. The strange thing was, yes, I had Unseelie ties now, but I didn't feel loyal to them. I felt faithful to myself, to my beliefs.

I guess I was my father's daughter after all.

Would the conclave let me continue working or scream conflict of interest? How could I support Mom if I couldn't work, let alone draw those bonus checks? I would have to give up my apartment with Mai and move back home, which would suck for all of us.

How could I leave Mom in a year when I had no idea how or if she could take care of herself? I mean, she could work, but she was settled into early retirement. She had no contacts in our area related to her old job, no prospects. Nothing but me.

"You are a wealthy woman." Bháin eyed me with bemusement. "Why work at all?"

"I'm not wealthy." Sweet as that dream was. "I'm just warming the seat of someone who is."

He cracked a smile at that.

Rook eased between us. "We should discuss your living arrangements."

"I have an apartment. I had an upstairs neighbor once." I narrowed my eyes on him. "You kind of remind me of him."

Rook had the grace to flush. "You must be protected."

"I will go with her." Diode's voice carried down the hall. "If you will grant me amnesty."

The flatness of Rook's lips led me to believe an argument was on the way.

I headed him off with a genuine smile for my guardian. "I accept."

"Thierry…" Rook warned.

"I can take care of myself," I told him calmly, "but I'll take Diode as a precaution."

He trailed his fingertips down my cheek. "I don't want any harm to come to you."

"I bet." I stepped out of his reach. "Wouldn't want to lose your regent status too soon, huh?"

Bháin touched my elbow, and a blast of ice-sharp pain shot up my arm. "We must hurry."

"He's right," Rook agreed. "The longer you wait, the more time we give your enemies to prepare for your arrival. If an attempt is made on your life, it will happen when you cross realms." Muscles bunched in his jaw. "Delaying your coronation will give you time to adjust, but you are at a greater risk in the mortal realm, where you are outside the protection of Faerie's laws." He appeared to debate what he said next. Those words came softly. "Seelie loyalists will stop at nothing to prevent your ascension."

I wished them luck. "Then you better get started on all those goals you wanted to accomplish."

A tic developed under his right eye. "Am I not allowed to worry about you?"

"Oh, I know you'll worry." I patted his cheek. "You'll fret every day I'm not under your thumb for you to press when you need some other impossible task completed, but you don't care about me." His mouth opened. I slapped my hand over it and scowled. "Don't go there, Rook. Just don't, okay?"

Turning to Bháin, I gestured toward Mom. "Let's do this. I want to go home."

CHAPTER THIRTY-ONE

As it turned out, leaving Faerie was even less fun than entering it had been. Mom wasn't drunk, but Bháin's reprogramming made her tipsy. He pumped her full of enough feel-good vibes she reached the tether convinced she was on an excursion in Chichen Itza to see the temple ruins. Bháin must have sent her cruising to Cozumel. That or her subconscious was hard at work explaining the jungle-like climate of Spring.

The way her eyes kept crossing as we trekked through Winter made me think that portion of the journey was a blur. She fussed when we put layers on her and complained when we took them off, but she kept rolling with the punches and never once lost the glassy stare making guilt simmer in my gut.

Ahead, the forest hunched over the remains of what resembled a stone arbor carved with detailed Celtic knot work. Thick pillars formed a neat circle while stout beams crisscrossed over their tops in a failed attempt at holding the encroaching forest at bay. The effect reminded me of wisteria back home. During the spring, it crept up trees and into houses, curling its tendrils into whatever the wind blew it against and claiming the space as its own. It was an invasive species in the south, a gorgeous pest with lush purple blossoms that hung like ripe grape clusters from elegant, verdant filigree vines.

I touched a curling green frond. "I didn't notice how beautiful this was before."

"You were too disoriented." Rook's wary gaze swept over the trees to the pillar then back to me. "We aren't alone. Grab your mother, and I will do what I can to hold them off while you cross. When you reach the other side, go straight to the magistrates. They hear all the gossip in Faerie. They know by now what's happened. They can help."

"Okay." After facing the High Court—twice—the magistrates seemed tame. "I can do that. This tether ties to the same spot as where we left, right? It will spit us out on conclave grounds?"

"There are surer routes in Winter and Autumn," he admitted, "but none are safe for you now."

"We should go." Diode prowled a circle around Mother. "Say your goodbyes."

Rook handed me the leather satchel Bháin had packed before we left Winter. It was filled with my newly acquired skins and some of Mom's belongings. I strapped it on and looked up at him. "It's been real."

He tilted his head. "Real what?"

"Eye-opening." I scuffed my feet, ready to go but having trouble leaving. "Do we hug or what?"

He eyed my knee. "You'll understand if full-body contact with you makes me nervous."

"Fair enough." I waved at him while I backed toward Diode. "You'll be in touch, I assume?"

Rook cleared the distance between us in two steps, hooked an arm behind my back and lifted me against him. His head dipped, those hungry eyes of his daring me to protest. "Sooner than you think."

His mouth feathered over mine, his unexpectedly tender kiss dragging a soft moan past my lips. That sound of encouragement had his grip tightening, his hands molding me against him. His tongue slid between my lips, hot and wet and reverent in a way that set a little warning voice screaming in my head.

I broke the kiss, twisting out of his grasp and crushing my eyes shut against the implications.

Diode's roar peeled them wide open in time to see him lunge at me. I dove aside, rolling over the mossy ground, shoving to my feet and bolting toward Mom. With her tucked behind me, I sought out Diode, who wrestled with a thorny snake. Made of vines, it hung from the arbor. It was thicker around than my waist and striking faster than my eyes could track. A second snake—or its second head?—hissed at Rook.

"Stay inside the arbor," he shouted at me.

"Not hardly." I didn't know how to work a tether. If that snake swallowed Diode or Rook, I was stuck here with Mom, and she wouldn't stay in her trance forever. I grasped her shoulders. "Stay put."

She blinked but offered no resistance. *Please let one thing go right.*

Shoving fear for her aside, I murmured my Word and peeled the glove from my hand. The snake raised a thick hood around its head. Venom dripped from its fangs. Its strikes came faster and faster.

No time to worry about them either. While Diode and Rook distracted the sharp end, I had to find its body. If I put my hand on it, I could kill it. Probably. I had never tried killing a plant, let alone a sentient one.

I shuddered. That was one skin I wouldn't be taking home with me.

Darting behind Rook, I ran into the forest and circled back through the trees until I stood in front of Diode and behind the snake. Its body was thick and scaly, its flesh the bright color of new growth. As I crept sideways, I tracked its movements until the vine wrapping the trunk in front of me flexed.

"Got you," I whispered.

Lunging for the base of the tree, I closed my hand around the vine and force-fed magic down its length. Mottled flesh turned black. Brittle roots pushed from the ground and hardened under my feet. The great snake coiled in on itself and died. Once it stopped moving, I jogged around the tree trunk.

I examined Mom, then Diode and then Rook. "Is everyone okay?"

Mom continued gazing at whatever image her mind's eye conjured for her. Diode shook out his fur then limped back to her side. Rook scooped pale blue gel off his face, revealing pocked scarring.

He caught me staring. "The venom burns, but I will heal."

"Thierry," Diode called. "Where there is one, there will be another. Thorn vipers nest in pairs."

"He's right." Rook wiped his hands on his pants. "Get inside and I'll send you home."

Home. I hungered for it so much the word made my mouth water. "What about you?"

His swollen lips twitched. "I'm surprised you care."

"Don't be." I huffed. "You helped sweet-talk the consuls into a twelve-month reprieve, which I won't thank you for— not because you're fae—but because this was your fault in the first place." I pointed a stern finger at him. "Be useful and do something about the other thousand-plus months left in the bargain."

As I stepped under the arbor and linked my arm through Mom's, Rook activated the tether.

The last I saw of Faerie was my fae husband's melancholy smile.

I couldn't sleep. After five hours of cross-examination by the magistrates, I ought to be exhausted, but I was wired. I still had a job. That was the good news. Whether they let me back into the field with my new status was up for debate.

They offered me an office job, but paper pushing wasn't my thing. I wouldn't last a week behind a desk, even with Mable for company. Plus, no bonuses.

I yawned long and loud, trying to fool myself into being tired. No dice. I was wide awake.

The night had ticked past in silence until I couldn't stand the quiet. I had to escape my apartment. As glad as I was to see Mai, my heart felt scoured. I was too raw inside, and not even her stash of Sweet Dreams wine quieted the chaos revolving through my thoughts. Rook, the Hunt, Mom, the High Court, Shaw, Rook, Macsen, the dead princes, Shaw. *Rook, Rook, Rook.* The mantra had pushed me into the elevator and up to the apartment over mine.

If the door had been locked, I might have gone back to my room. But it wasn't, and I didn't.

That's how I found myself taking comfort from the worn brocade couch Rook had abandoned in the same spot as where he conjured it, staring out his window into the calm dark of the sleeping city.

Mom was tucked into her bed at her house, sleeping off the hellacious vertigo she blamed on the cruise ship. Courtesy of the conclave, her yard was sporting a half-gnome bodyguard able to keep her property under surveillance twenty-four seven. Yeah, I laughed too until the cherubic lawn ornament quadrupled in size and lifted my car over his head...with one hand. Sven Gardener was one scary dude.

The sharp trill of my current ringtone had me patting down the cushions to find my cellphone.

"Hello?" I breathed against the screen while sliding it up to my ear.

"Thierry."

"Shaw?" My heart thudded painfully. He had been the one face missing from my welcome party. I even called him when he didn't call me. All I got was a canned message from his cell carrier. "Why aren't you answering your phone?"

"It's broken."

Relief that he hadn't been avoiding my calls slid over me. "What happened?"

"I ran over it with the truck. A few times. Once I heard you had been taken."

"It wasn't your fault," I said gently. "No one could have anticipated any of this."

"I should have made the case a priority. I should have checked my phone more often. I should have—"

"No." I pushed up straighter. "This was not your fault. None of it."

"I shouldn't have called," slipped out on a tired breath.

Feeling hurt, I growled, "Why did you?"

"I thought I could...but I can't. I might hurt someone."

My pulse leapt again. "You're hungry."

No answer.

I rubbed my left eye with the heel of my palm. "I'll tell security to let you up."

Apparently Diode wasn't enough to make the conclave comfortable. I had two new bodyguards. Mine were not as exotic as Mom's gnomian guard. I had been issued a standard pair of sword-toting sidhe warriors. Unseelie, naturally.

"Security?"

"I guess you haven't heard." I pushed to my feet. "We'll talk when you get here."

"Thanks, Thierry."

Don't thank the fae sat on the tip of my tongue. Fae. I wasn't all fae. I wouldn't trade thanks for favors. That wasn't me. I didn't know how. I didn't know if I could cash in markers even if I wanted to.

Tired of the caffeinated hamster running in the wheel of my thoughts, I swore. Enough semantics. I was too drained for this nitpicking, so I acted like a perfectly normal person and said, "You're welcome."

I hung up the phone before he got the chance to say more and padded over to the window. Whatever I hoped to see wasn't there, and my chest felt heavier for taking that final glance. The temperature had dropped since I arrived, and standing so near the tall window meant that my breath fogged the glass.

Afraid my guards might skewer Shaw if he beat me to them, I turned to go. My hand was on the doorknob when a tapping sound made me turn. Black against the night, a large bird sat on the windowsill.

Above its head, in the fading puff of my chilled breath, was written a familiar endearment: *a stór*.

A neat trick for a bird, especially considering the condensation was on my side of the glass.

I crossed to him and ducked my head until I was at his eye level. "I'm not your darling."

He fluffed his silky feathers and cawed once before vanishing into the darkness.

I don't speak bird, but I think his cawing laughter called me a liar.

A NOTE FROM HAILEY

Dear Readers,

When I wrote *Heir of the Dog* as the first book in the Black Dog Trilogy, I planned Thierry's journey to span those three novels and no more. But then I attended the RT Booklovers Convention, and all that changed. *Heir* won the American Idol Contest, and that brought two agents with fresh ideas into the mix. The next thing I knew, the trilogy had expanded to include one more title – *Dog with a Bone.*

Dog with a Bone is a prequel to the series in the sense that the novella cuts a hole into the ceiling of Thierry's past and gives us a glimpse of those first steps that set the events of the trilogy into motion one year later.

With that in mind, I hope you have fun meeting Thierry as a bright-eyed cadet in *Dog with a Bone* and enjoy watching her mature through *Heir of the Dog, Lie Down with Dogs* and *Old Dog, New Tricks* into a woman who knows when laws should be upheld and when they are meant to be broken.

Best,

Hailey Edwards

ABOUT HAILEY EDWARDS

A cupcake enthusiast and funky sock lover possessed of an overactive imagination, Hailey lives in Alabama with her handcuff-carrying hubby, her fluty-tooting daughter and their herd of dachshunds.

Chat with Hailey on Facebook, **https://www.facebook.com/authorhaileyedwards** or Twitter, **https://twitter.com/HaileyEdwards**, or swing by her website **http://haileyedwards.net/**

Sign up for her newsletter to receive updates on new releases, contests and other nifty happenings.

She loves to hear from readers. Drop her a line at **http://haileyedwards.wufoo.com/forms/contact/**

HAILEY'S BACKLIST

Araneae Nation

A Heart of Ice #.5
A Hint of Frost #1
A Feast of Souls #2
A Cast of Shadows #2.5
A Time of Dying #3
A Kiss of Venom #3.5
A Breath of Winter #4
A Veil of Secrets #5

Daughters of Askara

Everlong #1
Evermine #2
Eversworn #3

Black Dog

Dog with a Bone #1
Heir of the Dog #2
Lie Down with Dogs #3
Old Dog, New Tricks #4

Wicked Kin

Soul Weaver #1

Made in the USA
Columbia, SC
18 February 2018